Steinbeck: The Untold Stories

Steinbeck
The Untold Stories

Sixteen Stories
by
Steve Hauk

Illustrated by C. Kline

STEINBECK NOW

SteinbeckNow.com
Santa Clara, California

For more information, visit www.SteinbeckNow.com

Publisher's Cataloging-in-Publication Data

Steinbeck: The Untold Stories / by Steve Hauk / illustrated by C. Kline
ISBN 978-1546977315 (pbk.)
Fiction—California

Cover Concept: Dixie Layne
Interior Design: Marny K. Parkin

Address orders, inquiries, and correspondence to:
William Ray, Editorial Director
williamray@steinbecknow.com

Printed in the United States of America

For Nancy, Amy and Anne

Contents

Despite his fear, John refused to close the blinds. Often at night he went to the window and looked out, intentionally drawing hard on his cigarette so the embers illuminated his face, his graying mustache and half beard, his luminous eyes and receding hairline. He wanted to be seen in his full humanity, wearied but still creating, not beaten, a tough guy, an aging oak sheathed in strong weathered bark. —*"The Gaunt Visitor"*

Author's Preface

SEVERAL YEARS AGO, ON A DAY WHEN MY PLACE OF BUSI-
ness happened to be busy, a young man dropped a yellowed
copy of a handwritten letter on my desk, uttered a few words,
and left without giving his name.

An hour later I read the letter. Undated, it was from John
Steinbeck to Toby Street, a Monterey, California attorney and
close friend of Steinbeck's. Probably written in the 1950s or
later, Steinbeck wrote to Street that he had no home and that
depressed him.

It is the contention of these stories that John Steinbeck did, at
one time, have "homes"—California's Salinas and the Salinas
Valley, the coastal towns of Pacific Grove and Monterey, the town
of Los Gatos and the mountains above it. But he felt increasingly
less comfortable in them because of hostility for what he was
writing and, in one case at least, the threat of deadly violence.

These tales attempt to show, from a fictional viewpoint, what
that might have been like for him, while recreating the stories of
some of the people important to his life, both in California and
on the East Coast.

After the young man dropped off the letter, I received, from
another source, a copy of a 1942 New York State pistol license

application filled out by the author. Steinbeck wrote in the application he needed to carry a pistol for "Self protection."

Then letters written by Steinbeck to a Monterey policeman came in. In one, the author asked the policeman to ship the author's revolvers—presumably stored in Pacific Grove or Monterey—to Steinbeck's Manhattan address. In another, Steinbeck mentions a pistol, which he needed for house protection, and would the officer send that, too.

I might have marked all this off to a rampant gun culture, but encounters with different people over the years began to create a more provocative picture.

For instance, years ago a Monterey couple, an artist and a novelist, told me Steinbeck came to their home in 1934 and asked the couple to drive him to Salinas so the writer could see his mother, who was dying. This confused the couple because Steinbeck had other means of transportation. They finally understood when, on reaching Salinas, the writer ducked down in the car's back seat—he did not want to be seen in his hometown.

A Salinas shop owner named Lily told me another story of a dramatic episode, in the late 1930s, in which a gun was pulled on the author in a Salinas park. One can choose to believe her or not, but around that time Steinbeck applied for a California license to carry a gun.

Steinbeck friend and portraitist Judith Deim told me those in the Steinbeck–Ed Ricketts circle often protectively accompanied the writer on outings when there was a threat of danger. She depicted such a scene, of a pensive Steinbeck surrounded by friends, in her nocturnal painting "Beach Picnic."

When Steinbeck moved east he said it was because that was where the publishers were. While being in New York probably didn't hurt, he was a Pulitzer Prize-winning, best-selling author. Publishers would have considered manuscripts submitted by him wherever they came from. And he knew that.

Steinbeck moved back to Monterey with his family in 1944. He visited a friend's service station in Salinas one night but refused to leave the car, asking the friend to get into the car so they could talk. The friend told me Steinbeck had been concerned for his safety. Soon after, Steinbeck and his family returned to the East Coast.

The fact is Steinbeck put his life at risk writing on labor issues. He was developing a strong literary reputation for fair play, but one that potentially threatened his personal safety. Still, he didn't back down, writing what he felt was important. This took courage but must have extracted a heavy toll on him.

In that letter to Toby Street, the author spoke of wanting to walk by the tide pools again, that doing so was a good way to gain a sense of proportion. Perhaps he was thinking of Monterey or Pacific Grove. Of course, the Atlantic Ocean has tide pools, too. But to John Steinbeck, there was probably a difference.

John and the River

I DIED FIFTEEN OR TWENTY YEARS AGO, MAYBE LONGER depending on when you're reading this—after all, you don't stop remembering just because you're dead.

So I'm remembering a summer in 1914 when Alice and Mary and me wanted Mary's big brother John to come to the park and play some ball. Alice and Mary would watch though, come to think of it now, Mary could field and throw as good as most boys.

The thing was, John and Mary's mother Olive discouraged John playing with other kids. So John read a lot in the summer when most of us were having a good time or getting into trouble. Olive was not so strict with Mary even though Mary was a girl and younger than John. I think this worried Mary some.

Then one day Olive put the damper on even Alice and me playing with John. I guess we asked for it because we were heading for trouble for sure that day, though we didn't know we were, just being kids. It was that summer day I want to tell you about.

It was middle of the morning and for once the sun was out. You see, a lot of the time in the summer there's a morning fog in Salinas, which is the California town we live in. Olive was in the backyard gardening in a flowerbed behind John and Mary's house. We were watching her from behind an old oak tree. She wore a straw sun hat and canvas gloves. She was singing a hymn praising the Lord. We slipped around to the front of the house, hoping to find John.

As we figured, he was sitting by the parlor window reading, probably a story by Bret Harte, one of his favorites back then. I tossed a pebble at the window. John pretended not to hear the clink but we knew he had. So I tossed another and he looked up, kind of moody the way he could, and set the book down on a table. He came around to the front door and out onto the porch, softly closing the door behind him.

John was about twelve then and I was ten or so, and I should tell you at this time in our lives I was still almost the boss of John despite being younger. That's because I was cocky and John was clumsy and shy so naturally he was unsure of himself. For instance, when I walked to school, sometimes I'd look back to see John trailing behind me, if you can believe it. That was beginning to change by this time and sometimes to my surprise I found myself trailing after him instead.

"John," I said, tapping the mitt that hung on my belt, "let's go play some ball at the park. Mary and Alice will come with us and watch."

I said that softly so Olive wouldn't hear, you understand. To tell the truth, Olive scared me some. She was a schoolteacher so had seen most everything and seemed always to know what was going on. And she got things done so wasn't always patient with others. To give you an idea of her accomplishments, when we entered the war a few years later she became famous in our valley for raising hundreds of dollars for war bonds. I remember one day her talking to my mother thanking the heavens that both John and me were too young to go fight in Europe. Of course I didn't appreciate it then—I wanted to go fight, or thought I did until the bodies started coming home and there were funerals up and down the length of the valley.

"I can't play, Mother wants me to read," John said.

John peeked around the porch to see if Olive was near. You could catch just a glimpse of her shadow as she stooped over and dug and snipped and sang softly. "Anyway, I want to find out what happens to that old mule."

"What old mule's that?" Alice said in a smooth way she had.

"The mule in the story I'm reading," John said. "When Henry threw that first rock at the window I was reading the words, "The old mule had its nose in the air, picking up the scent of another animal, maybe a wolf.'"

Well, that was just like John, remembering the words and all.

"John," I said, "that's just a story! That's all it is! You come back in three hours—heck, you come back *in three years*—that old mule will still have its nose in the air for all the good it will do it."

"Maybe John doesn't want to wait," Mary said. "Maybe he wants to know what happens right now to that old mule."

John's little sister was always coming to John's defense, just as John was always coming to Mary's defense. They were best friends with each other.

Mary pushed her hands deep into her coverall pants and set her face in a way she had, something she did when she made up her mind to something. Mary was tough. She'd taken a fall and her pants were dirty on the knees and her hair mussed and it wasn't even lunchtime yet.

Alice said, "Your mother won't mind if you come do something, John. It's summer, after all. That old mule will still be there when you get back, just like Henry says."

John thought Alice pretty and this day Alice was wearing a lacey green dress that made her even prettier. I knew the way

Alice looked at John made him more aware of being awkward. You could tell by the way he looked away from her. I tried again:

"Come on, John, let's play some ball! Summer will be over in a few weeks."

"Henry, you know I'm not good at baseball," John said to me. "I'll probably be good when I've grown into my body. That's what Father says—my body has some catching up to do."

Well, that didn't make sense to me. I told John my body hadn't caught up either, but I was good at baseball anyway. Mary jumped right in:

"You're small, Henry, it's a different thing."

I didn't like hearing I was small, though I guess I was for my age, so I was glad when Alice spoke up and changed the subject.

"Who wants to play baseball anyway?" Alice looked at John again. "When a boy grows so fast like John, strange things happen to his body. Isn't that so, John?"

I knew John didn't want to answer because he started looking down, so I said, "If we can't play baseball let's cross the tracks to Chinatown, how about that? We can make fun of the old men."

Well, that finally brought John down the porch steps.

"I wouldn't mind going to Chinatown," he said, keeping his voice down. "But I wouldn't make fun of the old men, Henry."

"Because of the Tong? Because the Tong would get after us?"

I'd been reading about secret societies in the detective magazines and that included the Tong.

"Well, I don't know about the Tong, Henry. I don't think there are any Tong in Salinas."

"I don't care about any old Tong," said Alice. "I know—let's go on a picnic!"

"Where?" John looked at Alice and blushed, so he looked away and mumbled, "Where would you like to go on a picnic, Alice?"

"Somewhere there won't be adults telling us what to do, that's for sure, maybe down by the river. We can hide in the reeds and swim, and you know . . ."

"Swim naked?" Mary said suddenly.

Mary could just out and say a thing. Just blurt it out even if she might regret it. She was that way.

"Mary's not going to swim naked," John said.

Mary made a face and kicked at a rock.

"I wasn't talking about me, John! I wouldn't swim naked and I'll tell you why—snakes are coming out now! A hobo was bit down in the south part of the county. I wouldn't want to be bit any time but especially when I was naked. It was in the newspaper this morning. Father read it to Mother and me before going to work. The hobo jumped off the train from Los Angeles and camped by the river and was bit by maybe a lot of rattlesnakes, because there were bites on his arms and legs."

"I guess he must have been sitting down," Alice said.

We were all quiet for a moment.

"Well, it's true snakes are there," John said. "That's nothing new the last million years. They've been coming down to the Salinas River at least that long, way before people were getting in the way. Coming out of the hills to beat the heat and get water. If they can find any—in the summer the river's pretty dry. But if we're careful and Alice still wants to go on a picnic . . ."

"I don't know," I said. "If a hobo was bitten. . . ."

John said, "I don't think you have to worry, Henry. We're a long way from where that happened and the hills aren't so close to the river here."

"Who says I'm worried?"

"You're not?"

"Heck no."

"Good, so we can look for frogs and keep them for pets. There might be frogs hiding in the reeds. You like looking for frogs, don't you, Henry?"

"Sure, but so do snakes, I'd guess. And I'd suppose we have our own rattlesnakes here in Salinas, whatever you say about the hills."

"Well, if you don't want to. . . ."

"I didn't say I didn't want to. If you and Alice and Mary are game, I guess I am."

I knew I was trying to convince myself, so I said something else like, "Anyway, probably a lot hotter down in the south county than here in Salinas. So maybe there won't be any snakes here until it gets hotter like there, don't you think?"

"I think Henry's right," Mary said. "Mother talks about how hot it was when she was growing up in the south part of the county."

"Did your mother swim naked in the river?" Alice said.

"I don't think Mother would do that," John said, his face getting red again.

"They say the hobo's body was stiff and sprawled out, his mouth open and his tongue sticking out like this," Mary said, and then she stuck her tongue out.

"I don't want that to happen to me, no thank you. The newspaper said there was an open can of beans but the beans spilled onto the ground and maybe the snakes ate some."

John said, "Really? Did the newspaper say the snakes ate some?"

"No, I just thought it up."

Mary stooped to tie a loose shoelace, then stood straight.

"Honestly, John, who'd know if a snake ate a bean anyway?"

John thought about it, then said, "That's a nice story, Mary, beans and all."

"*A nice story?*" I remember Alice saying. "Someone's mouth open with his tongue sticking out isn't *nice*, John! I wouldn't want to kiss anyone with a mouth like that, would you?"

"Well, maybe his mouth wasn't nice," John said.

"His body stiff—*that* was?" Alice said stubbornly. You could tell she wasn't going to let it go.

"There's just something about the way Mary told it, that's all. I like the way Mary tells stories. She acts them out."

"I don't see what the excitement's about—she got it from the newspaper reporter."

"It was Mary stuck her tongue out, not the reporter."

You could see Mary was pleased John was sticking up for her. She put her hands on her hips and said, "I'm seriously thinking about becoming an actress someday."

John looked surprised.

"You never said that before, Mary, that you wanted to be an actress."

"I just thought it up."

"Well, I hope you do it. You'd be good."

I said, "I thought you said you couldn't go anywhere today, John."

"Going to the river's different than playing baseball and I'll tell you why, Henry. The Salinas River's one of the few rivers in the world that flows south to north. Another is the Nile River in Egypt! Flowing south to north must be important because the Salinas and Nile valleys are the most fertile valleys in the world."

"You read that?"

"Yes!"

"In a book?"

"In two books and a magazine!"

Sometimes John came up with stuff that knocked me over. I knew how many cylinders were in a six-cylinder car because I knew I was going to have a gasoline service station in Salinas someday. But I didn't know anything about the way snakes behaved or the direction that rivers flowed.

"So you're saying the Salinas Valley is like Egypt?"

"Well, we don't have pyramids, but when it comes to lettuce and strawberries, I guess so."

"Too bad we can't turn the other rivers in the world around and make them go south to north. We could grow more crops and make buckets of money."

John kind of rolled his eyes. He never liked talking about money.

"So I was thinking, Henry—so we can go to the river and look for frogs and watch the water go south to north—I was thinking maybe we could come up with a story to tell Mother."

We all looked to see if Olive was still gardening. We couldn't see her or even a glimpse of her shadow anymore, but we heard her humming another hymn. You could tell she went to the Episcopal Church and sang in the choir.

"A story so mother will let me go," John said softly. "I was thinking you could tell her you need to do a summer book report, and you want me to go to the library and help you select a book because you're only ten. You have to do a report, don't you?"

"Sure, but I was going to wait."

"Well, summer's almost over, Henry. You'll wait till the last day then wish you hadn't. Wouldn't it be better if I picked out the book and helped you now?"

I had to admit this made sense, so I said:

"And we'd really go to the river? That's what you're saying? That's a pretty complicated lie, John."

"Won't be a lie, Henry. We'll really go to the library. We just won't tell Mother the river part."

"I don't know—those snakes," I said.

"I'll bring a forked stick just in case."

"You know how to use it?"

"Sure—I've read up on it."

"In a book?"

"In two books and a snake manual—you put the stick on the snake's neck and pin it to the ground."

I tried to imagine John holding a writhing snake down. He's big so I could see him doing that, but then I said:

"Okay, but what happens when you take the stick off the snake's neck?"

"It slithers away."

"How do you know?"

"Wouldn't you?"

Not really thinking it through, I said, "Yeah, I guess so."

"Well, if you'd do it, why wouldn't a snake?"

"I don't know, a snake's one thing, your mom's another—she's a schoolteacher and smart. She sees right through me sometimes. Your mom's tough."

At that moment a shadow, humming softly, fell over us! John and Mary's mother took off her gardening gloves and pushed the straw hat back on her head. She was holding a basket with cut flowers. She smiled at us then looked at the sky, shielding her eyes. She'd come up on us as silently as the Tong. She said in a way as if talking to someone or something in the sky:

"I'm not so tough, Henry Henderson. Don't I give you oatmeal cookies?"

"Yes, ma'am!"

It was true, she did. She looked down at me, the sun forming a circle around her straw hat. If you'd seen it! It was like being in church and looking up at some figure with a halo painted on the ceiling like you see in books.

"And don't I tell your mother you are always welcome at our house?"

"Yes, ma'am, yes, you do," I said, hoping I sounded thankful.

"And don't you like my canned cold pickles?"

"I sure do—especially on a hot day like this."

"Well then, don't tell untrue stories about me. I hope you're not learning bad behavior from John. Sometimes John makes things up because he likes telling stories. You have to be careful with him. He didn't grow up on a farm as I did, so I wouldn't count on him being able to use a forked stick on a single rattlesnake much less a lot of them, as Mary tells it."

And she looked at John and then Mary. John's face turned red for the fourth or fifth time that morning and Mary pushed her hands deeper into her pockets and bit her lip.

"I do worry about you children. Why, hello, Alice! Aren't you pretty! Mary—Mary dear, look at Alice—do you see how pretty she looks in her green summer dress?"

Mary looked at Alice and then at her own dirty coveralls. Mary hated it when Olive compared her to other girls. She kicked at a rock but this time there wasn't one there. Mary kicked at things whether they were there or not. I liked that about her; I think most everyone did, even if they didn't know why.

"As you children know, I grew up on a farm down in the south part of the county. In the summertime rattlesnakes come to the river all the time. Why," she said, hesitating, "I lost my pet dog Buddy to a snake when I was just about the age of you children, so I learned a most painful lesson . . . I remember we found him all alone by the. . . ."

But Olive didn't finish what she was saying. She grew silent and picked up a flower from her basket and looked at it and I knew she did it because she thought she might cry. You knew she was remembering her pet dog Buddy and where she found him. I thought I might cry, too, so I looked away. Then she took a breath and said:

"I'm sure you heard about that hobo found dead from snakebite. He'll be given a pauper's grave with a simple wooden cross marking his place of rest. Our church will pray for the repose of his soul this Sunday. That hobo had no home, but now he will, and it will be with the Lord."

I remember she looked at each of us one by one with her sad eyes, and I knew she did it so we'd take in and remember everything she said. Then she pulled her shoulders back and said:

"Now Henry, now Alice, if you'll run along, please—to your homes, not to the river to swim naked. John and Mary have duties and studies to attend to the final weeks of this summer so they'll be prepared for the new school year. I'm sure just like always you'll all get together when school begins. Mary dear, help me in the garden, will you please?"

Alice took hold of my arm and we started to walk away. I knew my face was as red as John's, but I glanced over my shoulder anyway. Olive had Mary's hand and they were walking back to the garden, Mary carrying her mother's basket of cut flowers. John was climbing the porch in big steps, probably to finish reading the story of the old mule that had its nose in the air sniffing a wolf.

I remember hoping the mule's fate would be better than the poor hobo's—and better than ours, too. But then I think sometimes, even now, what if we'd gone to the river that day and there'd been a snake and it bit me or Mary or Alice or John, and one of us ended up like that hobo, only in a nicer grave? I think about that a lot, even now.

Burt and Jen

I

IF YOU WALK FROM WHERE THERE'D ONCE BEEN FISH PRO-
cessing factories in Monterey straight up into the hills, up a
mile or more through parking lots and yards until reaching Lot-
tie or Lobos streets, you've just about reached the crest of what
was once known as Huckleberry Hill.

It's all housing now, a mix of fishermen's cottages, flat-roofed
houses, sprawling apartment buildings and stone-and-redwood
architectural experiments with slabs of window overlooking the
bay and the processing plants below. You can still find huckleberry bushes here and there, usually sheltered modestly under
pine or cypress trees.

Once you're at Lobos you might even come upon Burt and
Jen's old house on the far side of the street. Well, not that house
but its replacement. The original house burned down twenty,
twenty-five years ago when Burt and Jen went off for dentist
appointments, which they scheduled together to save on gasoline.

It sounds contrived to say that their home insurance policy
had run out the day before the fire; too neat, too pat, too made-
up. But that's what happened, and when one looks back over
their lives, it's not surprising—Burt and Jen had fallen into a

13

disturbing pattern when it came to money and fire. Of the first, they had too little all their lives, of the latter, much too much.

Money was such a rarity that when Jen got a telephone call one day that a painting by Burt had sold for a hundred dollars, she broke into tears. Then she spent ten dollars on a cashmere sweater, deciding she would never again have a chance to squander so much money on herself.

As to fire, Burt's life was rife with it. In the 1930s a mural he painted with a successful older artist, a work so fine Burt thought he'd earned himself a touch of immortality, burned down—rather, the building it was painted on burned down, taking the mural with it.

A few years later he designed and built a theater on the wharf. Actors from San Francisco and as far as Los Angeles came to Monterey to perform on its stage before it, too, burned down.

As Burt moved into old age, a friend phoned to say that driving through a rural southern part of the county he'd come across a deserted old general store with a mural painted by Burt in the early 1940s.

Dimly at first, Burt began to recall and reconstruct this forgotten mural in his mind: a mission, monks in brown robes, Indians bent bundling wheat, ox teams tilling the fields. He recalled the joy of painting it, the sense of capturing the past, and most of all the exuberance of what had been his youth.

Within days, before his friend had a chance to drive Burt to see this forgotten work, a transient camped under the mural on a cold night, made a fire to warm himself, and burned the abandoned building to the ground.

So when fire destroyed the house on Lobos, Burt grieved for a time, then decided there was nothing to be done, it was destined to happen. This act of surrender made him feel better about failing to pay the insurance premium.

Besides, he didn't have the luxury of indulging in sorrow. He knew he had to rebuild for Jen's sake. He vowed his wife would not die homeless or, as bad, end her days in the little rented trailer home friends had moved onto the property after the fire.

Inspired, Burt became almost young again. He threw back his powerful shoulders and buckled on a carpenter's belt. There were newspaper stories about what Burt and Jen meant to the community and people wrote checks, organized fundraisers, held yard sales. Donations of plumbing, wiring, lumber and kegs of nails were delivered and piled up by the surviving foundation.

Friends showed up weekend mornings carrying tools and wearing new steel-toed boots purchased at the Red Wing shoe store at the bottom of the hill in New Monterey. Most of the helpers didn't know much about construction. But some, like Bill, who made his living as a housepainter, brought other skills to the job.

Burt was a gifted builder. If he constructed a floor, you could set a marble on it and the marble would not budge. If he joined two surfaces, they were flush. Though he loved art and literature, Burt came most alive with a saw and a hammer in his hands, and he knew it—he was turning tragedy into a personal rebirth.

Still, there were difficult times in the reconstruction. There were days of wind and rain and flooding of the grounds. Twice there were hailstorms. A falling cypress limb collapsed a wall of framing. Burt was beginning to feel like Job but continued on.

Jen, already depressed, felt hemmed in, the rain drumming on the trailer's tin sides and roof. When Burt asked a helper to fetch a tool from the trailer, the man was shocked seeing Jen, a shawl wrapped around her sagging shoulders, slumped in a chair, eyes hollow with despair.

The job was finished in a year and a half. Jen and Burt moved out of the dim trailer into a shiny new house featuring a light-filled atrium, floors of hard oak, a fireplace crafted of soft Carmel stone. New furniture purchased by friends made the house comfortable and inviting. A party was held and the wine flowed as it had in the old days of the marine laboratory.

Jen, able to bathe and preen, was once more poised and beautiful. Her eyes became bright and clear again.

His epic work completed, Burt slipped back into old age and died within the year. At his final request, people danced all night on Cannery Row in his memory. Like Burt, the party became legendary.

Jen survived him by almost a decade.

II

IN THE 1930s BURT AND JEN WERE YOUNG AND HANDSOME, a striking couple. Jen was tall and lithe with high cheekbones and a sensual mouth. Burt was square-shouldered, several inches over six-foot, with a wide face and broad sculpted forehead set off by thick, wavy hair.

They came to Monterey from Berkeley and the University of California. They were sure they would be wildly successful, Burt as a painter, Jen as a writer, and they couldn't have had a more auspicious beginning.

They met and charmed members of a talented artistic community led by Ed, a handsome, inspired marine biologist, and John, already on his way to becoming a major novelist. In return, they provided what services they could—services that sometimes turned into harrowing adventures.

There was the morning John arrived at their door and asked the young couple to drive him to Salinas. He wanted to visit his ailing mother, Olive. John had known Burt and Jen only a short time; they were flattered the author would ask them for a favor, much less confide in them.

Still, they were puzzled, because John had his own car. They found it awkward that John insisted on riding in the back of their old black Dodge, declining the front seat offered by Jen. John was tense so they became quiet, gazing out at the golden hills and dark oak trees on both sides of the curving road to Salinas.

Nearing the town, John said he didn't want to be seen, there were those in Salinas who wished him harm. Then he lowered himself prone to the seat.

When a sedan made a U-turn on Main Street and seemed to be trailing the black Dodge, Jen sucked in her breath. Burt prepared for possible battle, which excited him, his powerful grip tightening on the steering wheel. When the sedan turned off onto a side street, they exhaled, Burt partially in disappointment.

At John's direction Burt pulled the sedan around the back of a large Victorian house. John slipped out of the car and through the kitchen door. He climbed the stairs to his mother's room. He read to Olive, plumped her pillows, bathed her forehead. When she dozed off he kissed her cheek, returned downstairs, pulled the parlor curtains closed, and visited with his weary father.

John hid in the back of the Dodge on the way out of Salinas, then sat up and said:

"When I decided I would be a writer, I didn't think it would be dangerous. But I guess it's what you choose to write about. I should have written only about men and the land and left it at that, not man versus man. Mother won't live long. She's tired. Father, too."

Burt and Jen basked in the moment. Feeling safe, they took in the passing hills, the blue lupine and the cattle with their white faces. They knew he trusted them. They felt a strong bond with the writer.

A few months later, his mother dying, John disregarded threats to his person. If people wanted to harm him, so be it.

No violence happened and John saw his mother to her death. His father followed soon after.

III

B URT AND JEN HELPED OUT AT ED'S MARINE BIOLOGICAL lab when they could, typing reports, labeling specimen bottles, sometimes even washing Ed's clothing, salt-soaked from the hours he spent wading in the tidal pools.

To help make ends meet, Ed collected and sent specimens to colleges and laboratories throughout the country. One day, when Jen was helping with labeling, an order requesting live rattlesnakes came in from a laboratory developing snakebite serums. Ed knew of a place down the coast and asked Jen if she wanted to ride down with him; he needed money and wanted to fill the order quickly.

Soon they were in Ed's car heading for Big Sur. Ed had packed the back seat and trunk with burlap sacks and small cages, a few cold beers on ice, and cheese sandwiches made by Jen. It was a warm day—he wore short sleeves, Jen shorts.

They drove south on the coast highway, cliffs dropping off to the Pacific on the right. They passed Palo Colorado Canyon, crossed over Bixby Creek past Hurricane Point, then over the Little Sur River.

Ed pulled the car off the pavement onto a dusty road leading into the hills. He parked by a series of holes and clefts in dry brush leading up a slope covered with outcroppings of rock.

He sat back on his haunches and waved his hand over a cleft or hole. When a snake struck, Ed got his arm out of the way with the reflexes of an athlete, grabbing and pinning the snake with his other hand, depositing it in a burlap bag, returning to the car to cage it.

He was on his way back with a second snake when Jen screamed. He dropped the bag and rushed back—a large snake had fastened itself to Jen's naked inner right thigh, fangs buried deep. Ed yanked a folding knife from his pocket and cut the snake's head off at the neck, sawing as it whipped its body violently. The snake's head fell from her thigh.

He helped Jen to the car, sliced her thigh and sucked out what blood and poison he could, poured beer over the wound, tied an improvised tourniquet above it and threw the snake's head into the back of the car. They set off up the highway, driving several miles before either said anything.

"What did you do?" he asked.

"I tried to do what you were doing," said Jen, glancing down at the fang and knife marks on her thigh.

"Did you? Don't look at it. I'm afraid of shock. Do you feel dizzy? Feverish?"

"A little of both."

"You're very brave. A little silly, but brave."

"How much time do I have?"

He stared at the curving road.

"You'll be fine if we don't have a flat or something. And if we do I'll hail someone down. The hospital has rattlesnake serum. They handle these cases a lot. Goes with the territory. You'll feel like you have the flu for a few days, then you'll be fine."

He tried to say this in an offhand way, but his voice trembled, a kind of vibration echoing through his skull. After a few moments, she said:

"Was it a rattlesnake? It didn't look like one."

Ed looked over his shoulder—the snake's head was triangular and larger than a rattlesnake's. To Ed in his anxiety it looked the size of a garden spade. He found some comfort in its overlaid diamond pattern; that, at least, looked rattlesnake.

"Pretty sure it is. But could be something else, maybe nonpoisonous."

"I thought you knew everything there was to know about snakes," she said.

Jen was becoming feverish. She had trouble looking at the road, but didn't want to look at her wound again. She remained as still as she could, her legs tensed, her feet tight to the floorboard.

"No one knows everything," Ed said softly.

He could not tell her that he had never, in his considerable experience, seen such a snake in the flesh—or in a book, and he had read plenty on snakes. He wished he'd thought to toss the snake's body into the car, too. Right now he couldn't even recall if it had rattles. All he could see were its death throes and Jen's terrified face. Choosing the right serum would be a guess.

Why hadn't he had her stand at a distance while he collected? How careless he'd been. He wondered if the car would make it, if the tires were decent. He didn't look after it, just the way he was.

And whatever he said to Jen, he couldn't be sure a driver would stop for them if they did break down. Too, there had been rockslides along the highway. He worried about speeding cars on the dangerous curves. It was rare a month passed without someone driving over the edge, accidentally or intentionally. They crossed the bridge at the Little Sur River and rounded Hurricane Point.

It didn't help he was a little in love with Jen. Only a few weeks earlier he asked Burt to walk with him along the Pacific Grove shoreline. He said Burt and Jen should no longer come to the laboratory. He told him he was falling in love with Jen. Burt was devastated. Their lives were the laboratory and the people who frequented it.

Somehow Burt and Ed talked it out: that there were boundaries to be respected, but that it was worth trying to preserve the friendships. Ed knew at the time it was folly—and now fervently wished they had never reached such an agreement. If they had just gone their separate ways.

By the time they reached the hospital Jen was delirious. The doctors had never seen the head of such a snake, but rattlesnake serum was the choice and it was administered.

Ed had the head sent to a laboratory by express. He received a call the next day: the snake was a hybrid, a mix of rattlesnake and something else as yet undetermined. An unexplainable oddity of nature, the result of a sexual attraction between species.

Jen was ill for days. She carried the fang scars and was haunted by nightmares the rest of her life.

IV

JOHN SOON LEFT FOR THE EAST COAST, DRIVEN AWAY BY animosity and threats. He tried coming back from time to time, but it never worked. On a spring evening Ed's car did break down, stalling on the railroad tracks then hit by a train. Ed died in the same hospital he rushed Jen to years earlier.

As time passed, Burt became more involved in literature than art. But Jen was the writer in the family, publishing a pair of strong experimental novels. One book's tragic central figure had much of Ed in him.

Over the years Jen was quick to John's defense when locals said he had been nothing more than a drunk. "Oh, right," she'd say, "he was falling down drunk while writing all those novels and stories and winning the Pulitzer Prize. Imagine what he might've done had he been sober."

After Burt's death Jen spent her final years in a starring role. Beautifully garbed and made up, she appeared at events catered by the region's important hotels for the pleasure and favor of

guests who wanted stories and gossip of the region's romanti-
cized artistic past.

In addition to receiving money for her appearances—money,
at last—Jen's performance requirements were simple: a tall stool
that showed off her long legs, a Bloody Mary in hand. She told
stories of John, Ed, Burt and the others, often with a melancholy smile that gave the impression she was leaving something
unspoken.

That was something—the smile, the unspoken—the guests
spoke of often, as Jen knew they would.

The Elevator

I

THE NEWS CAME IN THE MORNING MAIL. HIS BOOK HAD been accepted for publication. The letter included a check, an advance. For the next few days John and Carol lived in a dream world. Everything was better: food, drink, sex. Their old arguments and complaints seemed less abrasive and were fleeting—a comment here or there and they'd smile and forget and forgive, settling back into the good feeling that had just come into their lives.

As to drink, Prohibition had recently been repealed so John and Carol didn't have to buy wine on the sly—driving to Monterey in the middle of the night as they had in the past, to a little garage where alcohol was available but trafficking was dangerous. They still had to go to Monterey if they wanted liquor because the town they lived in, Pacific Grove, had its own continuing prohibition on alcohol, shaped and enforced by a Methodist history and ethic. But during the first days after the letter, the trips to now-legitimate liquor stores, no matter how far, were a pleasure.

So too were the morning and early evening walks from their red cottage down to the shoreline tide pools. The water had a sparkle, the creatures scrambling in the shallows a special charm.

All life seemed fine and sacred to John and Carol—the urchins, the scrambling hermit crabs, the gulls, the lordly great white egret standing one-legged offshore on a gently drifting log.

John didn't write those first days. He tried but couldn't. He spent his time looking again and again at the publisher's letter. When he did set pencil to paper, he began thinking about his coming book. What would it look like? How would it feel? Smell? How many pages would it be?

And what artist would the publisher select to do the dust cover? There were plenty of artists on the Monterey Peninsula. Still, better not one of them for the job—could cause conflict, those not chosen would be hurt. He wanted none to feel pain when he was so euphoric. Better a stranger from elsewhere to create the cover. Besides, he'd had one book published, a failure, the cover by an acquaintance contributing to the disaster, at least in John's mind.

What about a foreword? The publisher's letter didn't mention that. But then, what could be written? "John such 'n such, an unknown writer with a failed book to his credit . . ." Not much of a foreword, he laughed to himself. No, forewords came after a writer had a body of work worth mentioning.

Carol continued her job as a secretary in a legal office, and while it was the same humdrum job, it was suddenly better because it wasn't forever. For the first time in a long time, she even thought it pleasant if uninspiring. More importantly, for the first time in a long time Carol didn't feel she needed to be inspired.

Daytime at home in the cottage, not having Carol to talk to about the coming book, John spent restless but happy hours in the yard, working off energy weeding and raking and, more meditatively, observing the fish swim or drift lazily in the little stone pond.

To kill time he wandered down the alley to the local department store to check the inventory of tools and gadgets. Or head in the opposite direction to the rustic marine biology laboratory down by the Monterey canneries to talk or have a beer with his friend Ed. When people doubted whether John had what it took to be a successful writer, Ed would say, "Wait, you'll see," and leave it at that.

Although John's first book had not been a ringing endorsement of Ed's confidence, its failure did not shake Ed's belief. Now Ed's faith in John would be tested again.

II

O N FRIDAY MORNING A TELEPHONE CALL CAME INVITING John and Carol to a party, a Monterey social event. It would be the following evening in an old Spanish adobe, the home of a beautiful dark widow. The caller sounded Mexican, perhaps, John thought, the widow's house manager or lover. The widow was known for parties mixing artists and writers with prominent citizens.

The invitation—though it was clear they were a last-minute decision—surprised John and Carol. Both were hesitant, but they talked about it and decided—because of the coming publication of John's book—being social seemed the thing to do. They cancelled a celebratory weekend road trip down the coast to attend the party instead, arriving late.

The man who called with the invitation met them at the door. He said his name was Lopez; he was handsome, self-assured. The widow Maria crossed the great room to greet them, warm with John, polite with Carol, making sure each had a glass of wine. She congratulated John on the acceptance of his book, surprising them. Maria told them everyone knew—and they found this to be true.

Mexican musicians played softly in a courtyard lit by candles and a central fire pit. John and Carol drifted out to the court-yard to listen to Spanish ballads and hide in the darkness. John didn't want to answer further questions about "the book." He was happy people asked, but felt he might harm the work by talk-ing about it. His responses were brief, occasionally curt.

A small man holding a beer stepped from the shadows. He wore a white shirt and dark tie, and there was ink on his finger-tips. Though youngish he was balding. He had an impish yet melancholy smile that drew people to him.

"Jimmy!" John said, happy to see a face he knew and liked.

"I heard you got an acceptance on the new book—and an advance, actual money they say."

"I haven't tried to cash the check yet," said John. "Too busy staring at it."

"You'll give me an interview?"

"Not my cup of tea, but for *you*. Let's wait until I know more."

"And I'll want to know what Carol thinks, too. She's important to your success."

"Yes, she is," John said.

"You're both happy?"

Carol said, "If you only knew."

"Good," said Jimmy.

Maria approached with a young woman, her daughter, and Jimmy moved off. Maria signaled Lopez. He had fresh glasses of wine delivered to John and Carol. The daughter, Tina, was

attractive with the dark hair and eyes of her mother, but slim-
mer and less voluptuous, something that would likely change
with age.

She was studying literature at Berkeley. She wanted to know
about John's book. Maria interrupted—she had someone she
wanted Carol to meet. It would only take a minute, and would
she come along? Carol gave John a questioning glance then followed the widow into the adobe. John and Tina laughed and
talked about writers who had influenced John from Thomas
Malory on. He asked after her courses, her professors, her family's history.

Soon alone as the party milled about her in the great room—
the introduction had been an awkward one—Carol watched
John and Tina through a window overlooking the courtyard.
Nothing was stopping her from returning and reclaiming her
husband, but she hesitated—she knew something in her always
seemed to court sorrow.

So she sat in a chair and observed them through the old adobe's thick windowpanes. Lopez sent over another glass of wine.
Carol knew she was getting drunk and didn't care. She also knew
that coming to this party had been a bad idea. If she could go
back in time she would have convinced John to say no to the
invitation. They should have taken the road trip as originally
planned. If they had, she might still be happy, still floating with
anticipation and hope. Now that seemed long ago.

Carol ran her hand over the wavy glass—it gave John and the
young woman a nightmarish quality in the flickering candlelight.
Their laughter seemed excessive, as did the way they looked at
each other, more so because they couldn't be heard. She felt she
was watching a grotesque film approaching a dark ending. Carol

looked away and thought of her life with John, of the jobs she worked to give him the time and freedom to write, the typing and editing, the arguments and battles and now, suddenly, with success in sight, this. She accepted another drink from Lopez. He looked down at her without expression.

III

JOHN FOUND JIMMY IN THE PARLOR.

   "Jimmy, I need your help," he said, leaning his head close to Jimmy's, taking him by the arm as they moved off. "Carol's drunk in the great room, almost sleeping, people giving her some leeway, thank God, so far no scene. You're the only one I can count on—I don't know these people, we shouldn't have come. Help me get her out of here."

   Jimmy set his beer on a table and followed John into the great room. Carol's eyes were half closed. The two men helped her to her feet, walking her slowly to the door, guests stepping back under the unspoken direction of Lopez who opened the door, bowing slightly with a muttered "Madam." On the sidewalk Jimmy offered to drive them to their cottage. John said that would make Carol think she could always get her way with him by getting drunk. She had done it before, he said.

   "I need to teach her a lesson, she drinks too much. We'll walk her down to the San Carlos. She wakes up in a strange room in the morning she'll realize what a fool she's made of herself. Do you hear me, Carol? . . . Carol? . . ."

   She reached out to touch his face. He turned away and they made their way clumsily down Calle Principal toward the hotel, Carol tilting toward the much shorter Jimmy. The hotel was in the Spanish style with a plaza and fountain. In the lobby a moth flit from lamp to lamp. John signed for a room while Jimmy helped Carol keep her balance, her breath on his neck. They guided her to the elevator. John propped her up in a corner, putting the key in her right hand, closing her fingers around it. She looked at her hand and the key, then at him.

"Room 327," he said to her slowly. "Go to Room 327, Carol— if you can."

Again she reached out to touch his face, again John turned away. He took Jimmy by the arm. They left the open elevator and the hotel and passed the fountain and made their way back to the party.

IV

JIMMY SLIPPED OUT OF THE PARTY. HE LEFT JOHN DRINKING, absently evading questions about the book, looking past his listeners. Jimmy found Carol crumpled in the corner of the elevator, door still open to the lobby, room key on the floor next to her open hand, palm up as if she'd been begging. If people had used the elevator they'd left her as she was. He spoke to her softly. With the clerk's help he got her to her feet, then helped her to the room on the third floor. He told her John would be along soon and she should sleep it off. He put her to bed, removing her shoes. He started back to the party, then changed his mind and went home.

Olie

I

OLIE STRETCHED HIS LEGS OUT ON THE CARPET, A PILLOW under his head. His mother Fran sat on the couch, knitting a sweater. Olie's pop Arne had just returned from his studio in the back, cleaning his hands with an old rag smelling of turpentine. Olie was used to that smell, had grown up with it because his father was an artist who worked in oil paints.

Olie stretched and yawned. It was summer, he was thirteen, and he could stay up late listening to the radio if he wanted. Tonight it would be *The Shadow*, one of his and his pop's favorites, though his mother would prefer a variety show, something with music and laughter.

"How's the painting going?" Fran asked, knowing how it was going influenced her husband's mood.

"Fran, why can't I do noses?" Arne growled.

"You can do noses. We've talked about this before. It's just the people you paint are fishermen and some of them have, well, different noses," Fran said.

"I guess that's it," said Arne. "I think fishermen sniff salt air all the time wanting to know which way the wind's blowing and if there's a change in the weather coming—their lives depend on it and it affects their noses, a matter of evolution."

Fran didn't know if she agreed with that.

"Well, they get them broken, too, don't they?"

"They sure do," said Arne. "Getting hit by a swinging boom or a giant flopping tuna can sure enough break the strongest noses."

He looked at Olie and then the radio. "Almost time?"

"Five minutes yet," said Fran, looking past her husband at the large clock in the kitchen.

Arne sat on the couch by Fran and, like Olie, stretched his long legs. Arne was a tall man, powerfully built. He had sharp blue eyes and dark eyebrows that swept up toward his thinning hairline, giving him a devilish, mischievous look, like a very large leprechaun.

Arne had studied art as a young man in Europe. To pay his way, he took jobs on fishing boats in the violent Baltic and North seas. Twice he saw storm waves sweep men off the decks of fishing boats to their deaths.

It happened first on a morning of frigid winds and icy rain. Before the boat could be turned to get back to the man, he had gone under, dragged down by his heavy rain slicker. The other time was on a moonless night when Arne himself was saved only because another fisherman grabbed him, pulling Arne back at the last moment. The man who fell overboard was not so lucky.

These deaths changed Arne as a person and as an artist. He saw how fragile life could be and he wanted to paint that. Fishermen, he thought, were a good way to do it. They risked their lives every day to put food on the table for their families. That seemed unfair, he thought—most people didn't have jobs that jeopardized their lives. Even a policeman didn't face danger every single day of work, nor a fireman.

So Arne began doing paintings of fishermen, their toil and the dangers they faced. When he returned to America, Arne decided to settle in a place where he could watch and paint men making their living from the sea. He chose the California town of Monterey, which had a large fishing fleet that plied Monterey Bay and the Pacific coast.

His paintings were good and he became famous in the world of art and sometimes beyond. When people looked at his paintings they felt his passion, the howling winds, the choppy seas, the lives in the balance. Arne was able to make a good living selling his art.

There were still a few minutes until Arne and Olie's radio program came on. Arne looked at his son.

"I saw Nino this morning. He said, 'Say hello to Olie for me, would you? He's a good boy.'"

Olie sat up. He liked Nino, an old fisherman who ventured out alone onto the ocean in his little boat Il Pesciolino, or Little Fish. The Monterey fishermen knew it was important to fish in groups so they could watch out for one another, so they seldom went alone. But not Nino—if something happened to him, there would be nobody to help. That was the way Nino wanted it, just himself, the sea and Little Fish.

His wife Zia would say to him, "My dear husband Nino, if you faint or have a stroke on the deck of Il Pesciolino, you could die of thirst and exposure before anyone finds you."

"My dear Zia," Nino would reply, "I would not be alone. God would be with me, He is Nino's friend."

Sometimes, when Nino came ashore after a morning and afternoon of fishing and had been too busy trying to catch fish to eat the lunch Zia had packed for him, he'd see Olie playing by the shore. He would invite the boy to join him on a bench to share his meal.

"Olie, I do not want Zia to think she prepared this lunch for nothing—she might not make Nino dinner!" he'd say. "So will you help me eat these olives and bread? And the cheese, too."

As they ate the boy and the old man would sit quietly and look out over the water and watch Il Pesciolino drift at anchor. Olie especially liked the sweet Italian cookies Zia packed for her husband. Nino asked Olie if he'd been good before giving him cookies. When they finished eating, Nino would tell Olie stories of the day's adventures, increasing the boy's desire to become a fisherman. The stories could be as exciting as a pod of orcas surrounding Little Fish, or as appealing to a boy as a drifting sperm whale lazily spouting water on a sunny afternoon.

Then Nino would struggle stiffly to his feet, pick up his burlap bag of what fish were left from what the markets had purchased, pat Olie on the head with his rough brown hand, and climb the steep hill above the harbor to his white cottage. From there he could look down at the harbor and see his little boat at any time of the day, at night, too, if there was a moon.

"Did Nino have a good catch today?" Olie asked his father.

"He did, Olie—but I'm afraid he lost most of it."

"Oh, no. How, Pop?"

"A seal jumped onto Nino's boat and ate a whole bucket of bottom fish. Nino said to tell you, five or six big ones. He knew you'd like the story."

"They must have taken him a long time to catch, pulling them up from so far down. What did Nino do?"

"Well, there wasn't much he could do, so he said to the seal, 'How much you pay to have this supper?'" Arne said, trying to sound like Nino.

"Nino said that?"

"Even so Nino said the seal stayed on the deck barking for more fish."

"What did Nino do then?"

"He said to the seal, 'How much you pay to have this ride on Il Pesciolino?'"

Olie laughed, then said, "Nino didn't shoot the seal?"

"No, Olie. Nino's rifle is only for scaring off sharks and beggar seagulls. Nino wouldn't shoot a seal. He loves everything, even the fish he catches and eats. That's why he blesses them."

Arne suddenly grew quiet. He liked his son was a friend of the fishermen, but he didn't want Olie to become one. He did not want to be afraid for Olie's safety as he was for Nino's and the other fishermen when the weather kicked up and the sea became wild. Or when a boat was late returning and the fishermen's families waited anxiously at the end of the wharf, praying to Saint Peter for their safe return.

"You see, Olie, fishermen don't make much money, so they must have a sense of what is important in life," Arne said.

"I know you think about being a fisherman, of loving the freedom of being at sea working for yourself, but it's a hard life. Not only is it hard to catch the fish, but as Nino's story shows you can lose them after you catch them if there are thieving seals or sharks about."

Then Arne switched on the radio, winking at Olie. "Anyway, it's time for *The Shadow*."

The program began as always with the sinister voice of The Shadow asking, "Who knows what evil lurks in the hearts of men?" then answering its own question, "The Shadow knows."

These words gave Olie the shivers. He wondered what evil really did lurk in the hearts of men. He knew his father and mother were not evil. Nino didn't shoot the thieving seal, so he wasn't evil either. Olie wondered if evil lurked in his own heart, and if so, did The Shadow know?

He remembered his father's friend John had come to the house a few nights before and was angry because some growers in the valley were paying field workers way too little, making them live in terrible conditions without shelter or clean water or even a place to go to the bathroom. And if they complained, they were beaten by policemen or hired thugs. John said that was evil, to punish a man who simply wanted fair wages for his labor.

Olie thought John had probably been drinking because he was using bad language. His pop said, "John, I agree with you, it is a bad situation, but you must not use language like that in front of my wife and son."

Fran said she'd heard worse from Arne's fishermen friends when something went wrong—like a net snagging driftwood or a shark eating a fish before it could be pulled on board. But she agreed that while Olie would eventually hear everything, there was no reason to hurry it.

Then Olie heard some words, seemingly coming from a great distance as if in a dream: "The weed of crime bears bitter fruit. Crime does not pay. The Shadow knows." He realized he had fallen asleep, because those words marked the end of *The Shadow*. He opened his eyes and saw his mom and pop smiling down at him.

"You missed a good one," Arne said.

"Not so good, Olie," said his mother. "It was better you slept. You've had a busy summer."

Then the doorbell rang. It was John, carrying flowers, which he presented to Fran with a bow. He said they were to make up for his bad language. He looked at Olie. "Son, I'm sorry for my language the other night. Your father was right to call me on it. Please forgive me."

Arne and John shook hands and went into the kitchen and sat at the table and drank coffee and talked about how difficult it was for working people to make a living these days. John spoke of the fieldworkers, Arne of the fishermen. They wondered who had it worse.

"One thing I've decided, John. I don't want Olie to be a fisherman. It's too dangerous. He will not be a fisherman if I can help it."

"You may not have to worry about that," said John. "I am hearing there are fewer and fewer fish to catch. My friend Ed tells me this. Have you heard the same thing from the fishermen?"

Arne nodded.

"Yes, I have. I worry. If the fish go away, the fishermen will go away too. I won't have them to paint anymore."

II

SEVEN YEARS PASSED. WAR BROKE OUT. JOHN MOVED TO the East Coast and then became a war correspondent in Europe. He wrote to Arne and Fran, describing events as he saw them and asking after Olie.

In Monterey, Nino died not alone at sea on Il Pesciolino, but in his bed, with his wife Zia sitting at his side, holding his hand. On his last night Nino asked Zia to help him to the window so he could look down at the little fishing boat bobbing in the moonlight. He thought of the many times he had taken it onto the bay and the wide ocean and how often he had come close to death. He thought for a moment he had already died and that made him feel unafraid and at peace. Then he made his way back to his bed for the final time.

Il Pesciolini floated in the harbor for many months. When she felt she could let it go, Zia sold it to two young fishermen. As she had when Nino was alive, she watched every afternoon or night for the return of Il Pesciolini. When the boat was late she worried about the two young fishermen. When it returned, she gave a prayer of thanks to Saint Peter, just as she had with Nino. It made her feel needed.

Olie did not become a fisherman. He went to college and when the war broke out he joined the Navy and was assigned to a destroyer. Arne and Fran talked about how strange life could be—Olie didn't become a fisherman but ended up on a boat on the Pacific Ocean anyway, at war.

"At least," Arne said because he knew Fran worried, "Olie is on a big ship, not a small fishing boat. He should be fine."

Then one day a friend of Arne's called from the naval station with chilling news. He said Olie's destroyer was one of several American warships closing with the Japanese. A great sea battle was expected any day.

Arne told Fran the news, held her hand a moment, then went to the kitchen and pulled a bottle of whiskey off the pantry shelf. He grabbed several packs of cigarettes and told Fran he was going to his studio.

There he put a large canvas on an easel, prepared his paints, choosing blacks, browns and oranges, white and yellow, picked out large brushes, opened the whiskey bottle and poured a glass to the top. He took a swallow of the whiskey, lit a cigarette, and studied the empty white canvas. He looked at it for a long time.

The only thing he knew for sure was it wouldn't be a painting of fishermen. Every few hours he'd nervously call his contact at the Naval station for the latest news. The two fleets were steaming toward each other, now separating and maneuvering for advantage, now coming closer, now separating and maneuvering. It seemed to Arne the Americans and Japanese were playing a game like chess, but the chessmen were real people.

Night and day Fran brought Arne sandwiches and hot cups of coffee on a tray. He barely touched the food. She did not look at the canvas on the easel. She did not want to see what he was painting. She had seen him this way before, and his passion frightened her.

When Arne got tired he slept in a stuffed chair. But he had dreams of the sea and the coming battle so woke quickly, frightened and shaking, his forehead covered in perspiration. He splashed water on his face. Then he'd light another cigarette. He'd have another whiskey or cold coffee and begin to paint again.

First he made great sweeps of black paint across the canvas, then splashed orange and yellow above the black. Close up it looked a mess, but when Arne stepped back the black became torn earth, the orange and yellow brush strokes fire or exploding bombs.

Out of the browns and whites and touches of black and orange a soldier appeared, dangling his rifle, his helmet pushed back on his head, dragging his boots through a field of bodies, some dead, some reaching out pleadingly to the soldier for help. The soldier's skin seemed to melt off his face, cascading down his neck and onto his brown shirt.

The soldier was tall and Arne thought he might be Olie, who had grown to be as tall as his father. But if it was Olie, why had he set the scene of the painting on land, not at sea? He did not know, but it did not seem to matter. He felt his brush had a life of its own, which was the feeling he had when he did his best work.

He made another telephone call to the Naval station. His friend was encouraging—the battle had been avoided for a time. Both sides withdrew to rethink the situation. Olie was safe for now, for a day at least the friend said. Arne should have been glad, but he knew that could change suddenly.

He felt a kind of anger growing within him. He thought about the times John had come to the house and raged about the treatment of the fieldworkers. He thought he felt something like John's anger now—that people had little say about events that determined their lives, that others decided for them.

He drank another whiskey and signed the painting with quick, hard strokes. On the back, in black paint, he wrote the word "War."

He left the studio and went into the house and told Fran that Olie was safe for now. Fran sat on the couch and put her face in her hands and cried. Arne handed Fran a handkerchief. He asked her how long he had been in the studio; she said it had been three days.

Arne thought about that. Then he stretched and went to bed and slept for a long time. He even slept through the bad dreams.

Lily

LILY HAD A LITTLE ANTIQUE AND JUNK SHOP A HALF BLOCK off Main Street. She also had a thick head of wavy white hair that she brushed up and back like a lion's mane. The store was as neat and clean as Lily herself, who shone with a healthy scrubbed look. Her strong jaw and high cheekbones were set off by distant, light gray eyes and straight white teeth.

Lily opened the shop shortly after her husband Len died from a stroke at age sixty-seven, and it became her life's center. She went into the shop almost daily to fill the loneliness; sometimes, if the sadness was upon her, opening on Sundays after church. Lily's shop traded in old furniture, tools and small farm implements, saddles and fancy bridles, quilts and framed vintage photographs from the Victorian era. Glass cases contained old post cards, yo-yos, Dell and DC comics.

On the counter she kept a plastic container of red licorice sticks for—as the handwritten sign said—five cents each. But when adults came in with children, she'd give the children a free licorice to keep them happy and allow their parents to browse. Anyway, she liked children. She even kept a full water bowl for dogs.

Now and then something valuable would come into the shop—a fine painting, a painted antique six-board chest, a rare piece of art glass, something like that. Lily was not lazy about researching such interesting acquisitions. If she thought it might be special but wasn't sure, she kept it in the back room until she was. After all, hardly a day went by that a runner or picker didn't stop in to hopefully pick off a valuable piece Lily had undervalued, thereby make a killing by reselling it in San Francisco or Los Angeles.

Lily acquired some of her inventory at yard sales and farm bankruptcy auctions. But most of the merchandise came through the front door with people in need of money toting items important and dear to them.

Oddly, there was one item Lily didn't want to see come through the door—books. She especially dreaded books by a particular author, yet they came in often because the author had not only been prolific, he had been born and raised—and so heavily read—in this very town, Salinas, in California.

Even if the seller didn't have a book by that writer to sell to Lily, the possibility one of his books might be among the offerings got her remembering again. That was something she didn't want to do: remember—it always led to a repeat of the series of nightmares that had haunted her so much in her younger years.

It was a telephone call that led to this dark incident, and it would stay with Lily all her life. To go back to a time in the late 1930s, there was to be a gathering, a reunion of thirty or so high school classmates. Two couples came up with the idea over too many beers at a bar in East Salinas; tipsy, they made late night phone calls, and the event was set.

The reunion was to be held in a town park on a spring Sunday afternoon. They would eat and drink and talk about what had been going on in their lives. The participants wanted the writer John to be a part of the gathering. He had, after all, been a member of their graduating class. But John had not been seen in Salinas for some time.

"He thought there were people in Salinas who might do him harm because of what he wrote and was writing, which is one reason he lived over on the coast. At least that was the story," Lily told a listener decades ago, just a few years before her death in the very chair in which she sat telling this story.

"To tell the truth, we felt John had deserted us for those snooty coast people and we were hurt. The folks here have long resented those people on the coast with their golf courses and big houses and ocean views while over here we lay down manure and grow most of their food for them. I can tell you the animosity was especially true in those days."

Lily was probably closing in on ninety at the time she told this story. She was sitting at her desk, the sun shining through the shop's front window, remembering. As she spoke, Lily absently watched the cars passing by.

"John and I had been close in high school, not sweethearts or anything, you understand, but we liked each other and kidded around a lot. We were both big, awkward kids, maybe that had something to do with it. He was a big fellow, I was a big girl. He called me Lil'. He was a funny guy, fun to be with, not so serious as people made out.

"Anyway, everyone said, 'Lily, you call him, you call John and tell him about our little get-together reunion, he will listen to you. You can talk anyone into anything.' And that was almost the truth—I can be pretty damn persuasive. 'If you tell him he should come, then he will. Remind him he was our class president and we want him here. It's only right.'

"So I called his house on the coast and Carol answered—she was his first wife, you know—and she didn't know me from boo.

She seemed pretty suspicious, maybe because I was a woman and everyone said back then I had a sexy voice, so someone who didn't know me might actually think I was pretty. Word was John and Carol were on the outs, or close to it. Well, she didn't have to worry about me. I was not pretty and perfectly happy with my Len.

"When I told her why I was calling she said she didn't think there was much chance of John coming to Salinas, but she put him on the phone anyway. He said, 'Hi, Lil', how are you?' He was cautious at first and that surprised me because it wasn't like the John I knew. But as we chatted he loosened up and we started talking about high school and that stuff.

"He even asked about Len and our kids and I asked him about his writing, which of course we had all been reading about in the newspapers anyway. He said to forget those stories, it was all balderdash, he was still struggling and, if he had his way, would always struggle because it was good for him. When I steered the talk to how things were going here in Salinas, he got real quiet real quick."

Lily paused for a moment, nervously rubbing her hands together. She continued reluctantly, not looking at her listener.

"Well, so then I got around to telling him why I called, you know, the reunion and all. He said right away, 'Sorry, Lil', I can't make it. Thanks for asking.' But just like me," she said ruefully, "I kept after him."

"I said, 'John, we all know you think people are mad here about what you've been saying and writing, about the fieldworkers and the working conditions and all, but we think you're imagining a lot of it. Sure there are some crabby people, a lot of old curmudgeons so dried up they can't spit, and some selfish growers just after the buck, but most of us frankly agree things need to be better. We don't think you should let the crabby ones keep you away. It's your home, too, after all.'

"Well, he still resisted, said it wasn't *that*, though I knew it was. So I played my whole card, I play to his ego. I told him we were all excited about his success and wanted our wives and husbands and children to meet the famous writer we'd gone to school with, and maybe at the same time he'd like to keep up with what all of us were doing.

"Of course nobody was writing anything about us, but most of us were doing okay. My husband Len's Western wear store was doing very well, for one. John was excited about that. He said, 'Good old Len, he has always had the eye. He picked you out, after all. You'll soon be rich, Lil'. I predict it.'"

Lily looked around the shop.

"Len's store was in this very space, did you know that? The place back then was called Len and Lily's Western Paraphernalia Store. Len picked that unwieldy name paraphernalia on purpose—he said it would encourage people to use their dictionaries. And once they got the word paraphernalia in their heads they'd always think of us when they wanted some of it. We did very well, so maybe he was right.

"When Len died I kept the space but it wasn't long before I turned it into this shop because I didn't like dealing with haberdashery wholesalers—that was Len's job. I've always loved old things anyway. Kept the same sign and had Western Paraphernalia Store painted out and Antiques and Etcetera Shop painted in so it says Len and Lily's Antique and Etcetera Shop. I figured people could look up etcetera just like they looked up paraphernalia. Anyway, etcetera covers a lot of things."

Lily tried to light a cigarette but her hands were shaking so she set the cigarette and lighter down on the desk.

"Len would laugh if he could see he's dealing in antiques now. Well, we still have some western things, like that hand-tooled saddle in the window, and now and then I buy a nice rhinestone shirt or beaver Stetson from a broke cowboy and heaven knows there are plenty of those about."

Lily stood slowly and walked to a worn, velvet burgundy curtain that divided the shop from a backroom. She turned and said, slowly and mournfully, "I don't know if I could count how many times I wish John had said no to me and hadn't made it to the reunion. But he didn't say no and he did come and you can't take any of it back once it happens. Amazing how long in life it takes us to figure that out."

Then she disappeared through the curtain, returning several minutes later carrying a shoebox tied up in string. Lily was breathing heavily. "I had to reach up high," she explained. "Need to buy a ladder."

Lily set the box on her desktop, snipping the string with a pair of scissors and pulling out a handful of old photographs. She handed them carefully to her listener.

"Those are photographs of the reunion. They're faded but you can still make out children playing tag or hide n' seek, adults drinking and eating. Must have been forty of us at final count. You can spot John in three or four of those, big guy with big ears, holding a beer. And he was happy when those photographs were taken—about his next book, about seeing people he liked, including Len and me I hope.

"I think the only thing he wasn't happy about was Carol. He hadn't brought her though we wanted her to come. Maybe he left her behind worrying for her safety. He knew there was a risk. But he didn't seem nervous like he'd seemed over the phone. I think those beers he had probably helped. And I think he believed me. I think he thought if I said it would be alright, it would."

Lily closed her distant gray eyes for a moment and said, "But it happened anyway."

"What happened?" the listener asked after a few moments silence.

"Well, the white truck," said Lily. "The white pickup truck happened. Came out of nowhere, a white Ford pickup truck. Jumped the curb onto the picnic grounds. A model with big headlights like cartoon eyes. You used to see those trucks up and down the valley. Everyone had one. I'll never forget those headlight eyes coming at us even though it was daylight and the lights weren't on. It seemed like a living thing. I think we all sensed what it was, especially John. The bastards could've killed a child. I think about that, what might have happened to a child all because of a telephone call I made."

"They were after John?"

"Oh, yes. Oh yes, oh yes. They must have known ahead of time. I always wondered about that, how they knew, still do. There were two of them, one had a gun, a revolver, threw John against a tree, the gun under his throat. Len moved in, some of the other men, but by then it was too dangerous, what with the gun at John's throat, so they backed off.

"The one without the gun, he said, 'You write one more effin word about fieldworkers and we'll blow your effin head off.' John's face was red and he was clenching his fists and we all yelled at one time, I don't know how it happened but we did, as if we'd rehearsed it for a week, 'John, don't move! Don't move a muscle!' Then Len stepped up and said, 'We know you boys, so anything happens to John. . . .'

"And they told Len he was an effin moron just like John. But they wouldn't have said that if they hadn't had a gun, no sir, and everyone knew it. Len would have mopped up the fairgrounds with them. Just to show they knew he could, they pushed John back and got in the truck and drove away real quick."

Lily's hands were shaking from the memory, but she lit her cigarette anyway and again looked out the window at the cars passing.

"So that's what happened more or less."

"Did Len really know them?"

"That was the inspiration by my Len. Nobody knew them. They were hired thugs, that's all. But Len put the worry in them. Maybe saved John's life."

"You notify the police?"

"We wanted to, but John said no, he didn't want us to, he already had enough troubles with crooks and growers and the law. Besides, the Salinas law didn't like him, and what were we going to say anyway? 'Two guys we never saw before in a white pickup truck like a hundred others? Oh, and officers, nobody got a license number either.'

"So we gathered our kids around us and sat quietly for a while, calming John with one more beer, him apologizing to everyone.

"Next day, a Monday, guess what John did? Applied for a gun permit—in Monterey, not Salinas."

"Did you ever see him again?"

Lily looked at him and then at the front door of the shop.

"Sure, all the time, honey. Still do see him in fact. See him in my nightmares on those nights after someone walks through that door with a pile of books. I'll see him tonight, for sure."

The Application

THE MORNING AFTER RECEIVING THE THREATENING PHONE call he went down to the Rockland County courthouse and picked up a New York license application that would give him the right to carry, concealed on his person, a revolver. He already had a pair of Colt automatics put away in the cellar. After the call, which came in the late evening, he immediately fetched one, loaded it and put it in the top drawer of his writing desk. Now that he felt he might need to use a weapon in defense, it would be a good idea to have the guns licensed.

A judge would grant or deny the request. With a courthouse clerk watching from behind a counter, John filled out the basic information with a pen: age, height, weight, race . . . the vitals.

For employment he did not say writer, but that he dealt in "information" for the U.S. government. His place of business was on Madison Avenue in New York City—not the house where he was writing and living with his wife-to-be, Gwyn, address House in the Woods, village of Palisades. To the question of had he previously possessed a gun license, he circled "Yes" and wrote "1938," when he lived in California. Then he looked up and saw the clerk watching him write.

"What is it?"

"It's fine you're filling this out now, but you'll need to take the application with you—the judge requires four character references before he can make a final decision."

John's eyes dropped farther down the form, "You're right, stupid of me."

"Each must be personally signed."

"I see that. Thank you."

What he had previously viewed as a mere formality now might be time-consuming, hardly automatic. Gathering character references could be difficult. He was suspected of Socialist if not Communist leanings. Even though he worked for the government—maybe because he did work for the government—he was watched closely and, he believed, followed. In California he'd had lifelong friends who vouched for him when he applied for a gun license. He had fewer friends in New York.

"By the way, you forgot to fill in why you need to carry a concealed weapon."

John wrote the words, "Self Protection."

"One tip: this judge looks more kindly on your application if you don't take too long collecting character references. Otherwise, he gets suspicious."

John tried to think of character reference candidates on the drive back to the House in the Woods. The list of close friends was short—he'd lived in New York little more than a year. He began making calls.

A novelist politely declined. He'd like to but he felt his new book would be controversial enough and didn't want to anger, well, he was indefinite about whom. A stage director said, "If times were different, I certainly would," adding too heartily, "We need to have a drink soon." John agreed, yes, they did, as he quickly hung up.

He had, meanwhile, repositioned the revolver in his desk drawer with the barrel pointing away and the hammer near the inside edge of the drawer. In this position he could grab the gun quickly with his dominant right hand. He practiced opening the drawer with his left hand, grabbing the revolver with his right. He moved his desk away from the window.

Gwyn, hearing him, pushed the door open and walked in, brushing her long hair.

"What are you doing? I thought you liked your desk there."

"I don't like my back so much to the window."

"Why the change?"

He didn't answer. She studied him for a moment.

"You haven't written anything for a while now. Are you okay?"

"Yes," he said.

"You're sure?"

"Yes."

Gwyn stroked her hair sensually. She thought to say something, turning her back to him as she spoke.

"Burgess called while you were away this morning. He asked where you were. I said I didn't know. He's in from Hollywood. Wants to know if you can join him for breakfast or lunch tomorrow. His treat. Just cast in a new film, said he's flush. Then Arthur called. He wants to talk to us about our next portrait sitting. He'd like it to be soon; he has some ideas."

"Gwyn?"

"Yes?" she said, turning back to him.

"Do you like the painting?"

"I don't know. I've thought about it too. It's dark but there's something I like, let's wait and see what he does," she said, leaving the room.

John now had the actor Burgess and the artist Arthur as character reference possibilities. He wondered why he hadn't thought of them himself. He checked the drawer to make sure the gun hadn't shifted when he moved the desk. He checked yet again to make sure it was loaded. He smiled to himself—a neurotic pattern was emerging. Then he called Burgess and they met the next morning for breakfast in a village diner.

When John asked, Burgess immediately said he would sign. John told him to be sure, that signing the application could threaten his career.

"What do you mean?" Burgess said, stabbing at scrambled eggs.

"I'm under suspicion. They think I'm a Commie, they follow me. You might want to think about it. These things make Hollywood nervous. You know that."

"You wrote the best role I've ever had. If I never work again I'll be remembered for it. I don't forget that. Who follows you?"

"Hoover's men, the FBI."

"You work for the government, what the hell are you talking about?"

"I'm telling you, Burgess."

John lit a cigarette.

"So what if you were a Commie?"

"I'm not."

"So what if you were?"

"You should think about it."

Burgess reached across the table.

"You ask me, everyone's nuts. Let me see that application."

Burgess set it flat, skimmed it, then pulled a pen from his jacket pocket and signed. Under business or occupation he wrote, carefully, the word *actor.*

He pushed the application back at John, smiled, picked up his fork and finished his eggs.

John found his second character reference an hour later—Morris, the family's veterinarian. Morris said he judged John's character by "the way you care for and treat your animals. Politics doesn't have anything to do with that."

As evening closed in John received two more refusals so remained two short. He would have discussed it with Gwyn, but didn't want to tell her about the threatening phone call.

Things were difficult enough for them, and they had been arguing. She wanted a child, he wasn't sure he did, not yet. His first wife Carol had also wanted children and he'd told her repeatedly it was "either babies or books." Carol would be wounded if he chose to have babies with Gwyn so soon, and Carol had been hurt enough.

It didn't help that during one of the portrait sittings the artist Arthur asked Gwyn when she was going to become pregnant. Gwyn smiled thinly at the question. John wondered if Arthur had somehow read their minds and was taunting them.

When he asked about it later, the artist said, "I'm sorry, it just slipped out. I try to think ahead when I paint, get underneath if you get my meaning, and for some reason I see Gwyn pregnant or, maybe, holding a baby and the baby is crying."

"You see me as angry."

"Stern, resolute," Arthur protested. "It's never going to be easy for you. I see that, so that's the way I paint it."

Gwyn wore a simple white dress for the sittings, but Arthur was painting it as a shift or slip, showing her spindly arms bare, her eyes distant and weary. John found something sexual about the picture, and wondered if Gwyn did, too.

"And Gwyn, Arthur?"

He shrugged. "She will need courage. It won't be easy for her either, will it?"

John knew it wouldn't, the strain was already evident. He decided to break off the subject. He didn't want people commenting on his writing until it was finished, and he felt a painter should be given the same freedom. He would wait to see the final painting.

A thunderstorm blew in off the Atlantic that evening and worked on John's nerves. He looked out at the wet windswept trees in the twilight. It was spring and the leaves were thick and the trees seemed impenetrable. For him the name House in the Woods had lost its charm. The surrounding forest, which had once seemed a refuge from the world, now felt like a trap. Someone could easily approach unseen through the trees. He checked yet again to make sure the gun was positioned correctly—and loaded. Then repeated the process. Then he laughed at himself.

The rain perversely made him think drought and drought made him think Dust Bowl and Dust Bowl made him think of Pare, a Palisades neighbor and potential character witness. Pare had proved fearless over the years. As a neophyte filmmaker he called out Hollywood for caving to corporate and commercial interests, then weathered an onslaught of criticism and career threats. Eventually he found he didn't need Hollywood—he had a president in his corner. With the urging and backing of Franklin Roosevelt he made a stunning documentary on the Dust Bowl, then moved on to a distinguished career of socially important filmmaking.

The storm cleared the next morning and John drove to Pare's house. His wife answered the door. She told John her husband was out of the country, but she would be happy to sign the application. Sally was enjoying a successful acting career on the New York stage. John asked her if she was sure; he told her a playwright crying career risk had turned him down.

She thought about it.

"Well, I'll be a little cowardly, I'll list myself as a housewife and property owner. Do you mind?"

John laughed to the contrary, housewives and property owners had higher status than writers or actors anyway. He welcomed it. He had one to go, and decided on the artist Arthur.

They met over drinks at a table in a small pub. John agreed to another portrait sitting, then asked the question, which Arthur mulled.

"Interesting," said Arthur. "Of course you know how colleges and universities can be."

"Not really, I was a college dropout," John said.

"Well, I teach at one, and they are guarded, it's inbred."

"Then you should think about it. I am being followed by Hoover's men and they could report you to the university, likely will."

The artist looked into his glass.

"You know, of course, that I also created a mural for the Department of Justice? I'm proud of it."

"You should be, it's wonderful work."

Arthur looked up, studied him as if he were an in-progress canvas. He wanted to see him as he would be.

"Why do you think they are following you?"

"They think I'm a Communist sympathizer. I'm one of many they think that about, though I don't know if we're all followed. Anything's possible."

"How do you know you're followed?"

"Sometimes I see them. Nice, clean-cut young men. It's odd, Arthur. I got a note from Hoover once, when I was still in California. He said while he was wary of my leanings, he respected me as a writer. He warned me to be more careful or someday my body might be fished out of the bay."

"Did you take that as a threat?"

"No, a warning—I felt he sincerely meant it and it turned out he was right, I was in danger. I sent a note back telling him thanks, but at the same time I was tired of his people stepping on my heels."

"What did he say?"

"To this day I haven't heard from him again."

"It's not because of Hoover's men you want to carry a weapon?"

"I wouldn't harm a federal agent, Arthur. If you want to know the reason, my life has been threatened, a telephone call I take seriously. If that worries you, don't sign."

Arthur thought for a moment.

"That does worry me—and convinces me. I've never known you to lie. The hell with academia."

He took the application from John's hand and signed it, thought a moment then listed himself as an artist, not university professor. John smiled. His character references included an actor, an artist, a veterinarian and a property owner.

The application was approved and notarized the next morning at the Rockland County courthouse. The photograph of John attached to the document showed him stern, resolute—not unlike, John realized, Arthur's developing portrait of him with Gwyn.

John carried the second revolver on his person, under his loose corduroy jacket. For a time, when he sensed he was being followed, he was relieved when he realized it was only one of Hoover's men.

Judith

JUDITH GREW UP IN THE MIDWEST, IN ST. LOUIS. HER mother gave piano lessons to children in the parlor. Judith loved to listen, music was in her blood. She'd dance to the simplest tunes by the students and sometimes her mother would play for her and be astounded by the way Judith danced, hypnotically like a serpent, her arms winding above her head, her body twisting and curving.

But while she would dance throughout her life, it was the print of a painting by Georges Braque hanging over the fireplace mantle that captivated her even more than music or dance. She loved the earthy colors, the bold planes, the flattened perspective and sharpened edges. The greatest appeal to her: the way the print could look like something one day, something else the next. Judith knew very early she wanted to be a painter.

So she danced and drew as a child, and as a young woman attended the St. Louis School of Fine Arts at Washington University. There she met another young artist, Ellwood. They found they shared a passion for modern art—he himself had grown up looking at a Fernand Leger lithograph hanging in his family's dining room. They decided that painting something directly as it was, or close to what it was, while fine for other artists, was not something they wanted to do. They wanted to paint the scene as they felt it or, if that wasn't working, as they wished they felt it.

Though Ellwood couldn't dance, at least not very well, they became art allies, then lovers, then married and set out from St. Louis on Highway 66 in an old jalopy, a wedding gift from Ellwood's father. They passed through the Missouri Ozarks and small towns with Biblical-sounding names such as Lebanon and Joplin and then into Oklahoma, where dust storms were desolating the land.

Free for the first time in their lives, they took their time, stopping in towns and farms along the highway or on side roads, visiting with people foreign to their experience, all hurting, all hungry. Judith discovered she had a natural empathy for the tired and struggling, so did drawings of the people when she could.

Judith also realized that the style she and Ellwood had developed in art school wasn't serving well her figurative drawings and paintings. So she changed it, making the figures she created more recognizable than she had at art school. If she wanted to evoke sympathy for the people they would have to look like people, she decided.

The sorrowful farmer, his face long and drawn, had to look like a farmer, but she discovered that she could remain faithful to her artistic philosophy by reducing him to the essentials and she did, making his coveralls a flat blue, his straw hat basic yellow, his hollowed eyes great dabs of brown.

Once she drew a very fat woman, which seemed odd, that someone poor might be fat in a time of hunger and depression, but there was greatness in the woman, too, and Judith recognized it—"Look at her, look how wonderful she is, all that fine fat," she told Ellwood, who nodded uncertainly.

Judith and Ellwood lingered too long in Oklahoma and by the time they traveled through Texas and reached New Mexico, sketching the life they saw along the way, they were running low on money and felt the pangs of economic depression sweeping the country. They had figured on five or six days to make it all the way to the coast; instead, in their second week they were down to a few dollars to buy gas for their jalopy.

With a sharp sense of urgency they hurried through Arizona and Southern California and reached Los Angeles, where they saw orange groves for the first time, then drove on to Santa Monica and their first look at the Pacific Ocean, at any ocean. On the beach they took out sketchbooks and did quick studies of the setting sun then curled up on the sand and slept through the night. In the morning they awoke to see a tall, barefooted man staring down at them and their drawings.

"These," he said of Judith's drawings as they sat up and rubbed their eyes, "look like something Braque might have done." Gesturing toward Ellwood's sketches, he asked, "Picasso?" Firmly, Ellwood corrected him: "Leger."

"Well, whatever inspired you, you are talented artists," he said. "Are you looking for work? Where did you study?"

The man, whose name was Gordon, was also an artist, an important one, and he'd been commissioned by the government to paint a mural inside a post office just up the coast. It was a federal project meant to get artists working, and Gordon needed assistants. He could hire anyone he wanted.

"Can you take direction well?" he asked. Ellwood said no, he doubted it, but Judith overruled him and said of course, they both could. She took Ellwood aside and pointed out they had only three dollars left and the jalopy tank was almost empty. So Ellwood changed his mind and said he could take direction well, though he knew he couldn't.

II

LIKE MANY OTHER AMERICAN ARTISTS OF HIS GENERATION, Gordon had been influenced by the Mexican artist Diego Rivera, and so under his direction Judith and Ellwood also painted in a somewhat realistic Rivera' style. This worked for Judith, because the human figure was becoming more and more important to her art. Ellwood still preferred geometric shapes and abstract symbols but he could do whatever was required, and do it very well.

Gordon worked them hard but they were glad for the job because so many people were unemployed. The irony was the post office mural showed men tilling fields, milking cows, picking fruit, tending assembly lines, fueling trains, when in truth jobs of any kind were scarce. Judith felt a touch hypocritical painting what she was painting.

Still, they felt fortunate to have work they liked to pay for shelter and food, with money left over to purchase more paint, paper, pencils, brushes and canvases for their own work. They were living an ideal California life that had disappeared for many, and they knew it. But Gordon hadn't mentioned a future project, and they also knew this mural could be the end of the good times.

One day, while working together on the same scene, they heard a deep voice behind them say, "That is fine painting you kids are doing. Were it only true that people could find such dignified work today." The man speaking was tall, blue-eyed, and calm; next to him stood a smaller man, dark and handsome, his hair swept back, his eyes downcast, his smile shy.

"What do you think, Ed?" asked the larger man, turning, hands on hips.

"I think it's wonderful art, but where are the fishermen?" Ed mused. "And where in the hell is a marine biologist?"

The large man was John, a writer. The small man, Ed, was not surprisingly a marine biologist. They were on their way to Mexico in Ed's car and had stopped to post letters. When Ellwood mentioned that he and Judith had driven to California through Missouri and Oklahoma, John began asking them questions.

"Tell me, did you talk to many people? Were there many on the road, heading this way? Someday I might make that trip, too," he said. Judith told him she had done drawings of the people along the route, and their hunger and sadness tore at her heart. Ed smiled softly and John nodded and said, "Yes, I can see you have a good heart."

"Look, kids," he said. "We have to make the border this afternoon, but if you ever come north look us up on the Monterey Peninsula, that's a few hundred miles north of here. It's a good place for artists. You'll find Ed's laboratory among the fish canneries—on the waterfront in Monterey. Can't miss it. It's the only building not made of corrugated steel."

A year later Judith and Ellwood arrived at Ed's marine laboratory. They had traveled up and down the state for months, working when they could, painting when they could, and they were ready to try something more permanent. Judith wanted children and a home.

Ed and John introduced them around town as talented artists who would contribute to the community. Judith and Ellwood rented a fisherman's cottage near the Southern Pacific Railroad tracks and sold an occasional painting, John and Ed sending prospective buyers to the cottage.

John telling stories and Ed's quiet charm and downcast eyes attracted Judith and Ellwood to the lab, which they visited almost daily. They were among many, the gatherings usually beginning in the late afternoons after Ed had finished hunting the tide pools and bottling and labeling the day's findings. Then he'd put a record on his phonograph, which he kept safely on a high shelf, and people would talk and drink and dance. Judith still danced as she did as a girl in St. Louis. To help make ends meet she and Ellwood answered the whistles announcing great catches of sardines, hurrying to the canneries to work long shifts on the assembly lines sorting sardines.

In time John saw that Judith and Ellwood's art was stagnating and told them they should go to Mexico to learn to "paint out loud." He gave them the money to do it from book royalties, so they did and were gone three months and nearly died.

At Lake Patzcuaro, in the state of Michoacán, Judith became ill and found herself in a fever on an operating table still dirty with pieces of flesh from a previous operation, a doctor standing over her with a hooked surgical knife. Though she often described herself as a mystical woman, but not religious, she deliriously bid the world goodbye and God hello.

Before the surgeon could make the first cut, Ellwood had second thoughts and dragged his wife off the table and they fled the country owing the enraged doctor many pesos. Days later they found themselves in Texas, and now Ellwood had the fever and raved like a lunatic, but opted for pills, not surgery.

When they started back toward California, floods hindered their way, rushing waters continually swamping their struggling jalopy at creek crossings. They putt-putted onto the Monterey Peninsula looking like the migrant fieldworkers John was beginning to write about, and when John asked if they had learned to paint out loud they told him they hadn't found a moment to paint at all, but certainly had a more vivid image of life. John said they would surely benefit from that and so would eventually paint out loud. Still not knowing what that meant, Judith and Ellwood ducked into their cottage and slept for two days.

They woke to the sound of the sardine cannery whistles announcing a large catch and calling people to work. Stumbling out into the light, they saw John and he said he had an idea.

"Listen, kids," he said. "I need to get back to writing. I haven't written a word for weeks. You both said you wanted to do my portrait. So instead of you packing sardines why don't I sit down to write and you sit down to do my portrait, so we'll all be working? I'll pay you more than you'd make packing sardines."

Not being stupid, Judith and Ellwood thought it a good offer, and though it was awkward at first, after three days John had written five thousand words, some of them good and some of them not, and Judith and Ellwood had finished portraits of the writer, and the work was good. Judith's portrait was modern with neat, clean outlines; it showed John contained and workmanlike, pen in hand, writing. John liked it.

Ellwood's was quite the opposite—it depicted John shaking, nervous and tense, his eyes wild and fearful. It was a psychologically interesting portrait but John didn't like it, though he didn't say so, not wanting to discourage Ellwood.

It could have been that Ellwood's painting had come too close to capturing something about John that John found disturbing. John paid them both handsomely anyway.

III

THE NEXT FEW YEARS WERE TENSE ONES FOR THE PEOPLE around the laboratory, including Judith and Ellwood. John was finishing a novel that some people didn't want published, and there was an undercurrent of danger everywhere. He'd had a close brush in Salinas, at least that was the rumor, and the group of painters, poets, photographers and other friends gathered protectively around the writer.

But the book did get published and won many honors. There were still threats on John's life, and he eventually moved to the East Coast. He wrote to friends that he needed to be there because that was where it was all happening in publishing, but his friends knew that was a smokescreen. At this point he was so famous he could be writing from anywhere and publishers would be interested. Ed still attracted people to the laboratory, but not having John's storytelling left a gap in the lives of almost everyone, including Ed.

Judith opened a studio gallery down by the canning factories and near the lab. Not long after, Judith and Ellwood, now with two children and Judith pregnant again, rented a larger house up in the Monterey hills on a street called Lobos. Their next-door neighbors were Burt, an artist, and his wife Jen, a novelist, a couple Judith and Ellwood knew well from the laboratory gatherings.

The couples got along well enough at the lab, but becoming neighbors put some strain on their relationship, especially because Judith liked sunbathing topless in the backyard. Both women were great beauties and strong-willed, but Judith was probably a bit too free spirited even for Jen.

Likes and dislikes temporarily went away when Ed's car stalled on the Southern Pacific tracks that cut through the canning district, and was smashed by a southbound train. Judith happened to be in her studio that evening and rushed to the scene of the accident at the Drake Avenue crossing, an abrupt rise up to the tracks.

After Ed was taken away by ambulance, Judith rushed back to her studio and, as she wept, painted a quick oil sketch she titled "The Accident." It showed three men and two women, palms not together but prayerfully leaning over Ed's stretcher. The figures were sparely sketched and noticeably elongated, a method Judith used when she wanted to capture a fleeting emotion. She caught a feeling of quiet stillness and respect.

John returned from New York and the old laboratory regulars came together in their grief, but after Ed's funeral and several days of private drinking back at the lab, John returned to New York and the group was never as close again, for the lab people seemed somehow abandoned.

Judith painted as much as she could find time for, often neglecting her children in the process. Judith and Ellwood's children were notorious for running around the neighborhood unwashed and causing trouble, and one of them would eventually cause so much trouble that Judith would have to leave the country, but that was several years down the line.

In the meantime she painted and read the works of the Spaniard Federico Garcia Lorca and the California poet Robinson Jeffers, who lived in a stone house he built with his own hands across the Monterey Peninsula in a village called Carmel. Judith was haunted by Lorca's recent death. In 1936 the poet and playwright had been brutally assassinated by fascist forces during the Spanish Civil War.

Judith loved Lorca's passionate poetry and plays and the news that such a kind and gentle soul was killed by a gun stuck up his rectum and then fired depressed her and made her feel at times mankind was of little worth. When one of her sons was accused of selling drugs, Judith blamed herself for not being a better mother, then fled to Europe with her two sons and daughter, leaving Ellwood behind. The marriage had gone bad anyway.

It was the early 1950s and she joined the Gypsies and the family traveled with them for a time. Judith did paintings of the people, and the Gypsies loved her art, for it seemed to capture them so well. Judith took to wearing silver bracelets and bright-colored scarves.

Judith's sons were growing into young men and caroused with the Gypsy boys and men. One learned to love and play the guitar. Judith's daughter Julia had inherited her mother's love for dancing, but soon surpassed her in technical excellence and artistry. Julia was becoming a great flamenco dancer, one for the ages, said her admirers, who watched her perform nights around open fires.

It was with sadness the family moved on, but Judith felt there was more for her children to see and learn, so they crossed the Mediterranean Sea into Africa. In Algiers the children saw a man stoned to death for stealing. Journeying into the interior, a pride of curious lions kept steady pace with their stalling car.

Judith told her children not to be frightened, something good would happen because it always did. And then it did, warriors with spears and shields trotting by, banging spears on the shields to keep the lions at bay, then escorting Judith's family to their village. Soon they settled in. Judith's sons learned to track and hunt from the village's young warriors. Julia learned to weave baskets and dance with the village women.

The family stayed a year then moved on to Spain, the land of the assassinated poet Lorca. Judith and Julia danced in tavernas in cities and small towns. On these evenings Judith attracted attention showing the painting or paintings she had done that day; when people gathered round she laughed then stood suddenly and danced. Even in Spain few had seen anything like Judith's dance but the people responded with warmth because they saw her rejoicing in it.

Flamenco was different, and when Julia stepped onto the center of the floor, or onto a small stage to join her mother, the stakes had changed and a critical judgment would be forthcoming. Judith and Julia circled a time or two, then Judith left the stage and watched her daughter enter into a world of great passion. People threw coins into a basket Julia had woven in the African village.

At a taverna in the foothills the family was greeted by Gypsies who had befriended them years earlier. Their people were camped nearby, on the banks of a descending, swift-flowing river. Please visit us tomorrow, they said, Judith and family joyfully accepting. Then the Gypsies sat back and watched Julia give her greatest performance, triumphantly stepping off a stage suddenly covered with roses, the African basket overflowing with coins.

The family joined the Gypsies' camp the next day. They drank and talked and when a small boy chasing a butterfly fell into the river, Julia, standing by the bank under a willow, dove deep, came up with the boy, pushed him onto the bank, and then was swept away. Her brothers and the Gypsy men dove in, and Judith, screaming insanely, splashed into the water in her long skirt and bracelets until she had to be rescued.

For Julia the strain of saving the boy had been too great, the water too swift, the boulders too deadly—her bruised and swollen body was found the next day downriver submerged under a jagged log. Judith swore she would never dance again and hoped in her heart that Julia, while standing that morning under the bank-side willow, had been thinking of her triumphant flamenco in the taverna the night before.

Julia was buried in the foothills near the river where she had died. Her mother and brothers returned to California and Monterey, but it was a mistake for Judith, if not the boys, now young men. In the early days of John the writer and Ed the marine biologist and the other painters and poets, Judith had been part of a group set apart—and thus united—from the rest of the community.

Now in her exotic Gypsy and African ways, in her beads and bangles and profound sorrow, she had set herself apart from the artistic community, too, and become, if not estranged, then not comfortable with them or they with her.

For they were now blending into the community, becoming respectable members of art associations or writers round tables or poetry corners or serving on art advisory committees. They had homes and mortgages and were settled, Ellwood among them.

Ellwood had lived quietly the years the family had been gone and continued to paint with some success, a gallery representing his work. He was glad to see Judith and his sons safe, but was broken by Julia's death for she had been his favorite; he could not help blaming Judith and he did not want to enter her world again.

Judith stayed nonetheless, opening a gallery in an abandoned metal building with broken windows and warped floors above the railroad tracks near where Ed had been killed. She replaced the windows, adjusted to the floors, but in time became restless. When word came the writer John had died in New York, Judith remembered what he had said about going to Mexico and painting out loud.

While the trip with Ellwood years earlier had been a disaster, Judith forgot the operating table and the mad doctor and remembered Michoacán only as strange and exotic, thus appealing to her nature. She sold what paintings and possessions she could, said goodbye to her sons, and left Monterey for Michoacán.

She found a crumbling hacienda in the hills above Lake Patzcuaro, a body of water where, the natives say, the line is thinnest between life and death. Judith decided for life and filled the house with canvases and brushes and pots and tubes of paint. She populated her paintings with harlequins and Gypsies and Africans, leopards and horses and dwarves, and sometimes, when a great sense of loss overcame her, a flamenco dancer, a young woman of great beauty and grace, her hands held high, her skirt swirling about her, a rose in her hair.

Judith called her work Magic Realism and it was fluid and prolific and dark so hard to sell but she didn't care. She simply wanted to paint, to somehow lessen the pain. Through her grief she was finally, she realized, painting out loud.

A woman from a near village came to help with meals and chores. Judith purchased a burro and cart. She took pleasure in petting the burro and feeding it hay. Just as she had attracted people to her table in the tavernas, life began to spring up around the old hacienda. Artists and poets and musicians from throughout the region were drawn to her.

In some ways Judith and Ellwood had become an argument for separation. Here they were, both past ninety, still painting, still creating, he in Monterey, she in Mexico. Toward the end Judith asked Julia's forgiveness for breaking her oath and began dancing again, as she had as a child.

Henry's Station

L IKE HE KNEW HE WOULD SINCE HE WAS A BOY, HENRY opened a gasoline service station on Main Street in Salinas in the state of California, when he was twenty-three years old.

It surprised a lot of people because Henry was always neat as a pin, and, other than cleaning windshields, which made sense for someone with his fastidious personality, few could imagine him doing anything like getting greasy under a car or changing tires, or even pumping gasoline.

Henry knew he didn't want to work for anyone else, but his options were limited: though smart he had dropped out of school at age thirteen when his father died, ending his formal education. He knew he didn't want to be a farmer or a cowboy, or work in the sugar beet factory that employed so many people from the community, so a service station seemed, if not ideal, then okay by him.

He signed on with a major gasoline brand and opened the place, calling it Henry's Service, and did well. Although he was accountable to a vast conglomerate, there was no one overseeing him, just an occasional stop-by and check-over by the conglomerate's regional inspector. Henry's Service, with its shining pumps, concrete pad you could eat off, and charming little station built in California bungalow style, always passed with flying colors. In fact, the inspector often wished out loud other dealers could match Henry's standards.

Henry liked routine. He opened at seven and closed at six, and he was there the full eleven-hour shift, Monday through Saturday. He had a mechanic, Bob, who unlike Henry finished high school and became certified to work on American cars, his specialty and passion being Chevys. So the ever-practical Henry drove a Chevrolet. Bob also worked six days, but the shorter hours of eight to five. In other words, Henry had no intention of getting under a car or, if he could avoid it, changing a tire. Bob did those things.

Henry could handle pumping gasoline, checking the oil and cleaning windshields, in fact quite enjoyed the last; if he couldn't see his reflection clearly in the windshield, he washed it again. He always looked good doing it, too, in a clean and pressed blue pinstriped service station uniform. He wore little white envelope-shaped hats supplied by the vast conglomerate, adjusting them at a rakish angle.

Henry brought his lunch to work, made and packed by his wife, Lorna. On foggy summer or cold winter mornings, Lorna, who came from an old Italian family in Monterey, would make minestrone soup and Henry would bring it to work in a little metal container; at noon he warmed it on top of the station's potbelly stove. Bob went home for lunch, which was fine with Henry because if people weren't driving in for gasoline, he liked sitting by the stove, reading a good book while having his lunch.

Henry liked mysteries, their neatness of plot and usually logical endings appealing to his nature as well as his vicarious love of suspense and adventure. However, if someone came into the station when Henry was reading, the assumption seemed to be it was a book by John, a well-known hometown author who every-one knew had been a close friend of Henry's when they were boys. Assumptions of this kind irritated Henry, as if he couldn't or wouldn't read anything by anyone but John. He didn't like being pigeonholed in this or any other way and couldn't keep his frustration to himself, not for a second.

"John is a very fine writer, but I read other people, too," he'd say before the conversation went further. "And since you bring it up, I'm probably responsible for a good deal of what John wrote. I taught him a lot about nature and people and baseball. He didn't know anything about baseball. He did know a lot about snakes, I'll admit, and the Salinas River.

"You ask him, he'll tell you what I say is true," he'd finish, knowing full well that would be difficult because John had been living on the East Coast and had not been seen in Salinas for some time and, having alienated many by what he wrote, was not expected to return soon. He wasn't someone you'd likely bump into on the way to the market or drugstore.

Still, Henry fully believed what he said, that he had been important to John's development as a writer. Regardless, he was alarmed one day to hear that John had returned to the area, having purchased a house somewhere in Monterey. Henry asked Lorna to have her family find out exactly where, and word came back John had bought an old Mexican adobe a few blocks from the harbor. He was living in the house with his second wife and his first infant son, and had, after a difficult search, found office space to write in on nearby Alvarado Street.

Henry thought about driving to Monterey on a Sunday with Lorna to visit John. But when he thought about it some more, he wondered why John hadn't visited him, or at least let him know he had returned. The more Henry thought about it, the testier he became. He would, he decided, perhaps never speak to John again. Henry, when you got down to it, had a temper, something John would have attested to, having seen it often when they were boys.

But despite his initial intentions, Henry didn't stay angry long. Henry never worried over anything too long; he found it unproductive. Besides, while he didn't believe the rumors, the talk of possible violence, he did know the town was an uncomfortable place for John to be, so he could be biding his time. Still, he *could* make a phone call, Henry thought.

Meanwhile Henry found himself remembering their childhood friendship. John's mother Olive for a time didn't allow John to play much with other boys, but she did like Henry, who lived next door. Though younger than John, Henry was initially the dominant personality of the two: John was insecure and self-consciously awkward, while Henry had every confidence in himself whether—and he realized this—warranted or not.

So Henry took the lead and felt protective of John, and he recalled walking to school with the older, much bigger boy awkwardly following behind. He smiled to himself as he remembered this, thinking how strange that must have looked, such a small boy being in control of such a big boy. To this day Henry thought that image, which must also have occurred to John, might have led to the creation of two of John's more memorable characters, a couple of itinerant farm workers.

Unlike those characters, as John grew into his body and began to find himself he became the stronger personality. Henry fought it for a time and could be stubborn and argumentative. He usually lost the arguments because John read a lot and armed himself with facts. Henry read too, but not as deeply as John, and the bigger boy usually outlasted him, amazing Henry in the process. But John admired Henry's spunk and remained patient and forgiving with him when their arguments became intense. When it seemed the charitable and smart thing to do, John would even allow Henry to have his way, to win the argument, especially after Henry's father died.

One night, after Bob had finished a valve job on a Chevy and gone home feeling good about his day's work, and Henry had locked the pumps precisely at six o'clock and was in the station gathering his minestrone container and lunch utensils into a paper bag and tidying the place for the next morning, a large gray sedan pulled into the station. Henry waved through the glass front door, impatiently signaling that the pumps were locked and the station closed.

But a man got out of the car anyway and tried the front door, which Henry had locked while counting his cash for the day. The man was black and powerfully built and Henry wondered a moment if he should open the door. But it was for only a moment, Henry having long ago decided that in this life nothing and no one would or could intimidate him, so he opened the door.

"Hello, sir," the visitor said, stepping back from the open doorway. "There is someone in the car who would like to speak with you."

"If anyone wants to talk to me they can damn well get out of the car and come up to the door as you have done," said Henry.

The man smiled.

"I was told you'd say something like that and I understand, but I beg you to please make an exception this time," said the man.

There was something about the way he said it, and about the general mystery and respect it implied, that got Henry interested.

"You mean he doesn't want to be seen? Do I know the person?" said Henry.

"Yes, very well," said the man.

"Let me see, I think it must be John," said Henry.

The man smiled.

"My name's Perkins," he said. "I know yours. Hello, Henry."

Henry, who had been angry for a time that John had not looked him up, was now flattered that he was taking so much trouble to see him, and taking what he thought was a risk doing it. And he was, after all, a famous writer, while Henry was simply the owner of Henry's Service. He looked out at the sedan parked by the ethyl pump.

"I wonder, could you turn out the front lights, please?" Perkins said.

"Yes, I suppose I could," said Henry, understanding what Perkins was thinking—suddenly cars driving by carried a hint of menace, especially if a vehicle slowed down. Henry was surprised how suddenly he felt this. He looked out at the traffic for a moment, a touch of defiance in his expression, then flicked the lights off from inside the door. He pushed his hat back on his head and closed and locked the door after him and followed Perkins out to the car.

Perkins opened the right back door. Henry got in and held the paper bag with his lunch utensils and minestrone container on his lap. John was seated by the opposite window, wearing a corduroy jacket and plaid shirt open at the collar. Henry could dimly see him by the street lighting, but more light was on the left side of John's face than the right, which was the side Henry was looking at. In what light there was, John looked much older and more tired than Henry had expected he would. He was unshaven and had grown a mustache. It had been how long, six years? Perkins shut the door and stood by the front of the car, his arms folded. Henry, like John, sat quietly and stared forward.

"It's a fine station, Henry," said John, still not looking at him. "I knew you'd get it when you said that was what you wanted when you were eleven or twelve."

"I was ten," said Henry. "You were twelve. But maybe I wouldn't have done it if my father hadn't died. Who knows what I would have done? That changed everything. I don't think you knew what you wanted to do yet."

John looked at him. Both were surprised at their formality. Then John's voice became warm and he leaned slightly toward Henry.

"Are you happy, Henry?"

"With the business? It serves its purpose. There are other things. Are you happy?"

"I don't know."

"Should you be here?"

"I wanted to see you. I didn't want to come and go without seeing you. I couldn't do that. But I don't want to get you in any trouble."

"I'll be fine. No one tells me how to live, you know that. You said you didn't want to come and go. Are you leaving Monterey?"

"I think I'll have to. There's more hostility than I had anticipated."

"Do you think you're imagining it?"

"I'm not . . . Henry, you know that Mexican adobe on Pierce I always liked, that I thought could be a dream home someday?"

Henry nodded. John was looking out the window now, so Henry felt silly nodding. John turned back to him.

"I bought it, but there's too much history. Something dark happened in that house, I can feel it. And whatever it is, it's engulfing us. Gwyn feels it too. Something very heavy, a murder or suicide. Something like that. Terrible suffering. And I don't mean ghosts. Ghosts I can handle. I have a ghost, no problem. He travels with me. Irritating at times, but we've found a way to co-exist. This house though, there's an evil there worse than any ghost."

John waited but there was no reply. They were still not comfortable with each other. There was a time Henry would have launched into a conversation about ghosts or evil from a pragmatic point of view. Not now.

"Am I keeping you—do you have to get home? Will your family worry?"

"Sometimes I stop for a beer," Henry said. "So I get home maybe twenty, thirty minutes late sometimes. I'm fine."

John held his wrist up to the window and peered at his watch.

"I'll keep the time. I think about us a lot. Cigarette?" he said reaching inside his jacket.

"I don't."

"I remember when we tried our first by the river. Mary was with us. You got sick."

"We saw a bloated cow floating in the water that day, flies everywhere, remember? Maybe that was why I got sick."

"Yes, could have been. I know I never thought of the river the same after that myself."

Henry waited a moment before speaking again.

"Why did you take the chance of coming back?"

"Couldn't let the bastards dictate my life, Henry. Got a call from them in New York, back a bit. Said though they were three thousand miles away they were thinking of coming after me. Now they know I'm close by, but whether they want to come into

Monterey . . . Well, I have some protection. I'm not a martyr, don't believe in it. George—you remember George?"

"Yes."

"A cop, as you're probably aware. They're keeping an eye on the family right now, George and the Monterey cops, or I wouldn't be here."

For a second time, Henry felt flattered. "I understand," he said.

"But if it makes you nervous us being here, then I would understand and we'd drive right out of here, we'd go immediately."

Henry laughed.

"What?"

"You sounded like your character Lennie—'I'll just go away, George.'"

John laughed. "I did? Yeah, I guess I did. You think I'm becoming my stories?"

"Maybe."

A car pulled into the station. Henry stiffened and watched, John leaned forward, dragging nervously on his cigarette. Henry wanted to warn John the glow from the ash illuminated his face.

With Perkins turning and watching, the car slowly backed up then went forward, back out onto the street in the opposite direction. They were quiet for a moment, watching the taillights disappear into the darkness.

"Do people do that, pull in after you close?"

"To turn around? All the time," Henry said. "You're working on something?"

"Yes, but it's supposed to be comic, and I'm not feeling comic. But comedy's better with some tension, so who knows . . . I'll tell you something, Henry, the threats, that stuff, not as bad as . . . doesn't hurt as much as. . . ."

"Yes?"

"Well, it took me two weeks to find someone who'd rent me office space in Monterey. Down on Alvarado, where I spent so much time back in the thirties, vacancies everywhere. But nobody 'knows me' anymore, or if they do where are my references? Or the space is vacant and for rent, yes, but it's promised to . . stuff like that, all bull. One guy I knew a long time says, 'Big deal if you win some awards for writing.' I didn't bring up any award—I don't care. Where the hell did that come from I'd like to know."

Another car slowed in front of Henry's Service, then moved on. Perkins opened the driver's door and looked into the back seat.

"John, I'm feeling uneasy about this. We're pretty obvious sitting here, station closed and all," he said. "Hell, the cops might stop to check on us and you don't want that."

Perkins got back into the driver's seat, closed the door, and put the key in the ignition and started the sedan.

"Just to keep the car warm," he said, looking over his shoulder.

"Perkins is a great pilot and a hell of a driver but a terrible liar," said John. "We'd better go."

Then he looked at Henry.

"Be careful, Henry, don't stop for a beer."

"Don't worry about me. I may not be popular, but my mechanic Bob is. No one would touch me if they value getting around this town."

Henry gathered the bag with the lunch utensils and minestrone container. John patted his shoulder and Henry looked at him as if they were kids again, trying to figure him out. He never had.

Perkins waited until Henry drove off in his Chevrolet. Then the gray sedan pulled onto Main, heavy with homebound traffic, then west on the quiet curving highway to Monterey. A few miles down the road a car approached swiftly from behind then stayed close to the gray sedan. Perkins kept an eye through the rearview mirror, his body forward, foot tense on the accelerator.

Then Perkins sat back and laughed.

"It's Henry's Chevy."

John laughed too.

Slim

M Y FIRST GLIMPSE OF BEAU HE WAS TUCKED INTO A corner of his shop, which was sunlit because San Miguel, a little town in California's Salinas Valley, gets a lot of sun.

Beau was leaning back on his chair so the top was pressed against the wall, reading an old hardback book almost touching his nose, smoke hovering over his head. Beau was wearing jeans and a blue and white plaid Western shirt with pearl snap buttons. The heels of his black cowboy boots, scuffed and aged almost to gray, were hooked on the chair's bottom rung. His dark hair was speckled gray and his blue eyes, when he peered over the top of the book to look at me, had a faraway and flinty look that was at first alarming then, the flint softened by a thin smile, charming. He was slim, couldn't have been an ounce of fat on him.

I guessed him to be sixty, sixty-five at the time, a tough, hard sixty or sixty-five, but then his age was hard to gauge because he was a cowboy, or had been, you could just tell even if he hadn't been wearing a shirt with pearl snap buttons—he was gaunt and his skin was brown and leathery like a cowboy or farmer.

In a rough way Beau was striking in his looks and presence; handsome and distinctive-looking; I thought a better-looking

Warren Oates, if you remember that fine Western film character actor. Or maybe Ben Johnson.

"Browse away and help yourself, friend," he said, knocking the ashes off an unfiltered cigarette. "Today's your lucky day, first person steps in, and that's you, gets a free paperback book."

"Is that a policy?"

"I just made it up—one of the perks of having your own business," he said.

Then he nodded toward a bookcase that was near a table with used-for-sale clothes draped over the top, jeans and shirts and a couple sweaters. The bookcase had four shelves of books, hardbacks and paperbacks. The books were probably the highlight of the shop, because to be honest most of the stuff was junk.

I guessed the cigarette Beau was smoking was a Lucky Strike because there were several opened packs of that brand lying about, as there were three or four ashtrays. One read "California Rodeo, 1947" on the curving side and if you looked through all the ashes and butts you could make out on the bottom an etched in glass cowboy holding on to a bucking horse, his hat whirling into the air.

"Not for sale," Beau said, watching me stare at it. "Everyone wants to buy that one, minus the cigarette butts of course. I turned down twenty bucks couple years ago when twenty bucks was more like forty today. I competed in that rodeo."

"Did you win the ashtray?"

"Didn't win anything that year and it was my last rodeo. Got bucked on my ass in front of my girlfriend back then and seven thousand other people. That wouldn't have been so bad but the horse stomped all over me and broke my leg in three places. I didn't cowboy for another five years, and from then on, when

I did, I cowboy'd badly. Couldn't sit a horse more than a couple hours and hold the tears back, still can't, and no cowboy can make a living that way. You can sing on the range but you can't cry. It's not seemly. Bought the etched ashtray because I had a strong feeling it was my last rodeo.

"Anyway, maybe that wasn't such a bad thing. Rodeos began going to the dogs in those days—hell, that year in Salinas they introduced something called wild cow milking. Whoever heard of such a thing?"

Beau seemed so disgusted I thought he'd spit, but instead he gazed out the window of his shop for a moment, getting a faraway look I would come to recognize as Beau's melancholy mood, then said, "Course almost no one sells ashtrays for souvenirs anymore. So maybe mine's not worth much after all. Seems everyone's afraid of smoking now days."

"You're not?"

"Nah—I enjoy it, young fellow," he said, perking up. "You can bet something else will get me long before smoking does. For instance, something like this but more so—take a look if you have the stomach for it."

Beau rolled up the right sleeve of his plaid shirt. His forearm was scared and deformed, the muscles seemingly torn away then patched back over with skin that had an unnatural shine to it like it had been turned inside out, and maybe it had.

"Looks like a grizzly bear took a chunk out of me, don't it?" he said. Beau stared at the old wound as if seeing it for the first time. He touched it gently with his left hand.

"Still tender. Always will be. Or maybe that's just me imagining. They say skin's got a memory. Ripped out the muscle. The doctors connected my wrist and bicep with some sinews and a strip of muscle from my rear end. Can't do this anymore because of it," and he grabbed a book out of the top shelf of the bookcase and gestured with it, indicating a tattered dust cover illustrating a couple men in a field harvesting some kind of crop.

"Can't do what?"

"Well, buck grain bags, like the hands do in this book, *Of Mice and Men*, by a man named Steinbeck. You ever hear of him?"

That seemed an odd question. I said I had.

"I'm finding most people have," Beau said thoughtfully. "You see, I never was much of a reader. I'll have a story for you sometime about that. Anyway, used to find this kind of work when I couldn't get a job herding cattle, but since the injury the strength in my right arm is not much so that's out too. So I opened a place like this in Paso, but nicer, that went bust. Too much rent. Then this place, rent's almost free in San Miguel these days things are so bad."

"Paso?"

"Paso Robles, down the road. First time in? I don't recall you."

I said it was and asked him how the forearm injury happened.

"Well, you drove down from the north, did you?"

I said I had.

"Thought so. Then you passed the oil fields by San Ardo. That's where it happened. I hired on working those oil fields, grunt labor, stopgap job, saw a stone on an auger, reach down to lift it off and some supposed skilled labor idiot turns on the auger. Ripped my arm up. They stopped the bleeding, flew me in a helicopter to a hospital up in San Francisco. Never passed out though they thought I would. So here I am crippled up and running a shop. By the way, my name's Beau."

We got to talking about a lot of things, about antiques and cowboys and Beau himself. He said he grew up on a little horse ranch outside Paso Robles—or Paso, as he referred to it. Said the family lost the ranch in the Depression, and so his mother and father moved into Paso to spend their final days in a cramped place without plumbing or electricity on a road called Vine Street. Though he talked around it, I got the feeling Beau's father had been broken by the times, couldn't make himself begin again so drank away his last days. Beau being a natural athlete, he set out on his own to be a cowboy, working on ranches and, when he could afford the entry fees, competing in his youthful passion, rodeo.

He said he was looking for work when he met Steinbeck near Jolon, which is in Monterey County. Beau said John bummed a cigarette from him, but he felt that was just a way to begin conversation, because when they sat down to talk John pulled a pack out of his shirt pocket and supplied the cigarettes himself. Beau said he didn't know when that was, maybe around 1935 or so, when Beau was barely into his twenties and, like almost everyone else back then, searching for any kind of employment he could find.

He said he'd come into Jolon in the San Antonio River Valley to hire on for a month or so of herding. He said he and John sat under an elm tree outside a general store where the road divided and you could take it one way to King City or another to Mission San Antonio or another over the mountains to the Pacific Ocean. Beau said he only realized a few years later it was Steinbeck he was talking with, and that only from reading newspaper stories and seeing photographs and thinking back, because the man never said a word about writing or being a writer, just wanted to talk about that part of the county and Beau's job of herding cattle. Beau said he told John about farm work, too, because he also hired on for that during those difficult times though he'd rather not have.

"I told him how you could throw your back out loading bags of barley onto wagons or throwing around bales of hay," he said. "And I always thought cowboys weren't made for that kind of work because of our bowed legs, but you get what work you can.

"Other than that, can't tell you anything earthshaking about him. Just told him it was all tough work and at the end of the day a man could drink a gallon of beer just to get enough liquid back into him, and there was nothing more important than being a part of your horse if being a cowboy was what you did. And so years later I made myself useless for even that."

I waited a moment.

"Did you like him?"

"Sure, guess so, but as I told you, I didn't know who he was then. It was after he wrote that book *Grapes of Wrath* and his picture started appearing in the papers and he became the subject of a lot of talk in these parts that I realized who I'd been talking to."

"Did that talk make a difference how you thought of him?"

"Well, I had to think about it for a time because an awful lot of people hated his guts, you know. I even heard some farmers' group had a contract out to break his legs. So naturally I wanted to know why. A few liked him, weren't many. Myself, I didn't see the harm in telling the truth and that's what it seemed to me he was doing more or less. Hell, who knows the truth anyway? Then I didn't think about it anymore, had the rodeo accident and the auger accident and opened the place in Paso and then this place and started reading to pass the time. It can be pretty quiet and pretty lonely for long stretches in a place like this. Anyway, he became one of my favorites along with Jack London."

"Why was that?"

"Why because I was familiar with the terrain he described like in this book. I know every hill and stream and gopher hole between Paso and Salinas—well, think I do—and it seems so did he, convinced me anyway. Now go ahead and pick out your paperback. I need to open up some shelf space for incoming inventory."

I found a nice little paperback edition of "My Name is Aram" by William Saroyan, surprised to find it in a shop in San Miguel, but then Saroyan liked California valley towns, coming from one himself. The pages were brittle and yellow from acid burn so it would have to be handled carefully or it'd fall apart. Beau lit another cigarette, smiling I'd found a book.

II

SAN MIGUEL'S MISSION STREET IS THE TOWN'S MAIN AVE-nue and it runs parallel to a railroad line. In the old days it was part of the highway but now you can bypass it and most do, leading to the tough times. If you enter town on Mission Street from the south, the first thing you see is the mission with its bell tower of five bells and its vast U-shaped courtyard and adobe walls.

Built by the Franciscans in 1797, Mission San Miguel has seen the murder of a family living within its walls. It's been secularized and returned to the Catholic Church. Damaged by earthquake and restored, it's the only mission left with its original fresco paintings. These exquisite works of art were painted by the Salinan Indians of the region under the direction of a Monterey artist and dealer in cattle hides and tallow named Esteban Munras.

After you pass the mission the part of San Miguel on the left side of the road takes on a ramshackle character of indifferent homes, a tiny park, a small post office, a diner or two fronted by boardwalks, a place that sells used appliances, and a resale shop better organized than Beau's run by a gentleman named Mr. Pinion who bears an uncanny resemblance to W.C. Fields, right down to the bulbous nose and dancing eyes. The other side of the road's a grain elevator, a train station and wide agricultural fields leading to the base of dusty foothills to the east.

Despite the poverty there is something inviting and seductive about it all, the heat and the dry wind and dust that blow up the valley and through the town, and the silence, which gives every sound added meaning—a screen door slamming, a voice singing, a called greeting, even Beau's smoking cough. You kind of want to settle down into one of those simple houses, pour a glass of wine or something stronger and just be quiet and listen to the small sounds of everyday life, make it that simple.

I developed a pattern of stopping in San Miguel and visiting Beau's place two or three times a year. Beau's was on Thirteenth Street, a side street off Mission. The road dips down from Mission Street and then up to the highway. Beau's was on the left side of the road near the bottom of the dip and just across the street from a little white church staunchly claiming its place in a mission town.

Beau's shop had no name though fragments of faded lettering on the front windows indicated it had once been a Chinese laundry and then a few things after that. Beau didn't seem to think he needed any kind of signing, that people would look in the window and figure out what kind of place it was and that was probably so.

Beau mentioned once that he didn't like being on a street named for the number thirteen. He said San Miguel in his mind and the minds of some others was a bad luck town, stemming from the brutal 1848 mission murders of a family of nine and an Indian sheepherder and a black cook from Philadelphia—and how did he end up in San Miguel?—stabbed and bludgeoned to death by renegades that had been hospitably invited to tie up their horses, have something to eat and spend the night.

That, and a plague of spinal meningitis that overwhelmed the town a century later from a nearby military base, and the fact that San Miguel had seldom known prosperity outside the Franciscans in their good times, and that he himself was there, convinced Beau the town was unlucky.

Beau said it was nice that visitors might fantasize about living the quiet life in San Miguel, and that it was true a recognized photographer once said he drove a hundred miles every few weeks to a San Miguel diner for "fried eggs and a side order of peace and quiet," but the reality of it was another matter and that, frankly, in his opinion the town was haunted.

And then Beau, coughing, lit up another cigarette.

III

ONE DAY I GOT A LETTER POSTMARKED SAN MIGUEL. Coming from there it had to be from Beau, of course, though he was the last person I expected to receive a letter from. He scrawled in a shaky hand he'd made "a find that wasn't junk" and thought it would interest me, though it was something, he wrote, he positively would not sell, to me or anyone else.

The only hint he gave me was the find was related somehow to his favorite book. I thought about what that might be over the next few weeks, until I could arrange my schedule to make it to San Miguel. I decided it probably had something to do with *Of*

Mice and Men, because he spoke of the book often, and surprised me on one visit by wondering if the author had modeled the character Slim in part after him.

"I don't know why I think that, but he wrote the book after meeting me, and every time I read it I think Slim is me," he'd said to me. "Or at least a small part of me," he added softly

"And if things had worked out better, if I hadn't broken my leg in three places then lost half my arm in the oil fields, maybe I would have been a foreman like Slim, and like Slim I would have been fair with my men. I would have liked a life like that. That would have been a life worth living."

When I walked through the door the shop was empty; Beau sometimes walked down to one of the diners for coffee, leaving the door unlocked. But that wasn't it. A moment later Beau came out of the back room with a tall woman he introduced as Beth. She was combing her thick red hair and Beau was buttoning his cowboy shirt, and neither seemed embarrassed or ill at ease by my presence. Women liked Beau, and he liked them. Most of his visitors were women, and as he said, the shop could be lonely.

"It's about time you got down here," Beau said.

Beth found her purse and excused herself after giving Beau a peck on the cheek, saying she had to get back and grade "a passel of high school English papers. See ya', honey."

Beau grinned, signaling to me that Beth was okay, then ducked into the back room and returned carrying a large framed picture. Well, it wasn't exactly a picture. Beau set it on top of the bookcase, stood back and lit up a cigarette and smiled broadly.

"Well, what do you think?" he said.

Under the glass was a black and white double page magazine ad for Ballantine Ale. But what was striking about it, looking out thoughtfully at the reader, holding a cigarette in his fingertips, was John Steinbeck's mustached face.

"Found it at a yard sale in Paso. Surprised the hell out of me," Beau said. "Found it late in the day, around two o'clock, anyone could have picked it up before me. But no, it waited for me, so must be fate. Probably Life or some other magazine, 1940s maybe. I haven't taken it apart, haven't taken the back off yet."

I'd never seen Beau look so proud. The ad was clearly related to *Of Mice and Men*—the background was a painting of men gathering and loading hay, and the ad copy, likely written by Steinbeck himself, sounded like a parody of a scene from the novel.

"'The sun is straight overhead. There isn't enough shade to fit under a dog.'" Beau read to me mock-dramatically. "'The threshing machine clanks in a cloud of choking yellow chaff-dust. You wear a bandana over your nose and mouth, but your throat aches and your lips are cracking.'

"But this here is my favorite, I've memorized it—'Let's say the boss is a man of sense and humanity. He comes bucking over the stubble in a jeep, and on the back seat is a wash boiler of crushed ice and bottles of ale. Such a boss will never lack for threshing hands.'"

I looked at Beau, who was grinning again.

"Who's that *humane* boss, huh?" said Beau, putting emphasis on humane. "He had to be thinking of Slim, and maybe, way back in a corner of his mind . . . well, you know, maybe me, from that conversation we had back then in Jolon. I'm sure he recognized I was humane the way I talked about cowboys and you got to love your horse and care for livestock. Some find, huh? Like my rodeo ashtray, I'm never selling it."

Well, I felt I had an obligation to make an offer and when I did, his grin just got wider.

"Knew you'd want it, but sorry," he said.

IV

I DIDN'T SEE BEAU AGAIN FOR ALMOST A YEAR, JUST NEVER had a reason to get down his way. When I finally drove back into San Miguel I wouldn't have been surprised if Beau's had become something else, maybe a laundry again.

But it was still Beau's place. I could see him inside, standing stiffly over a table, managing some inventory, some hand tool pieces, hammers and such. But there was something strange about the scene and then I figured it out—Beau wasn't smoking.

Of course he *was* wearing a cowboy shirt, this one a pale blue that set off his eyes, which had a strange kind of watery shine to them. He'd lost even more weight—couldn't have been more than a hundred and twenty–five pounds and, one hand on the table, seemed to have trouble keeping his balance. He turned shakily to greet me, smiling almost shyly.

There were no packs of Lucky Strikes anywhere. His rodeo ashtray seemed to have disappeared too. He spoke immediately, anticipating me, but softly, his voice raspy like he didn't have much breath in him.

"Well, friend, I did it to myself, just like entering that rodeo in Salinas in '47, or reaching down into that auger in the oil fields. Funny what we do to ourselves. Don't need any help messing ourselves up, do we? It's one thing we're good at. Comes natural to us. Well, to me anyway.

"So, few weeks ago . . . Beth had just left . . . lit up a Lucky . . . coughed up something sudden like . . . brown, lumpy blood . . . landed right in my hands. Kept my head like with the auger in the oil fields, wouldn't let myself pass out, put it all in a plastic bag, drove to this hospital south of Paso. Doctors said there was no doubt what it was—a part of my lung, a little chunk of my lung just broke away when I coughed, if you can imagine that.

"I overheard one of the doctors in the corridor say I was a living autopsy, bringing up a piece now of what they would see later.

"I know what you want to ask but are too mannerly. Another doctor, he said, when I asked the question you're thinking, 'Sorry, Beau, I'd be lying if I didn't say your chances are pretty slim.'"

It was a full year before Beau's space was rented again, that's how slow it was in San Miguel back then.

Big Lizard, Little Lizard

I

JOHN AND JOANNA INVENTED THE GAME THE DAY BEFORE. IT grew from memories of their childhoods. Excited, they shopped for prizes for the competitors-to-be and came up with children's cowboy and cowgirl hats and red, blue and white woven lariats.

The next morning, the Oldsmobile's trunk packed with the prizes and their suitcases, they left Los Angeles before sunrise, driving north on El Camino Real. The morning light, reflecting off the ocean, took hold around Ventura and John switched off the automobile headlights, stretched and leaned back in his seat.

In Santa Barbara the traffic picked up. They stopped for coffee in the little town of Buellton. John spotted pearl-handled penknives in a hardware store, purchased a dozen as additional award gifts for the children who would be competing in their contest, plus one each for his two young sons Thom and John back east. He added another for Elaine, whom he hoped to see the next day at his Pacific Grove family cottage, and the last for himself.

"I was pretty good at mumblety-peg," he told Joanna as they got back on the highway.

"Were you?" She smiled.

Joanna had large blue eyes, dark eyebrows she used to pow-erful theatrical effect, sensuous lips and one of the best-known faces in America. She wore jeans, a Western plaid shirt, her hair swept back dramatically.

John had been nervous since they left Los Angeles, submerg-ing it in their chatter of the children's camp they'd be visiting later that day. Joanna smoked, looking out the window, asking questions. John mumbled his answers. Sometimes he would leave her questions hanging. She tried to read his mood.

"What's the matter, John? Thinking about Elaine?" Joanna had promised Elaine she would look after him. Joanna realized few women in America would trust her to look after a man, all the more reason she was determined to do a good job.

"That, yes, but we'll be crossing into Monterey County in an hour."

"Why does that make you nervous?"

"I don't know. Don't you get a little nervous when you go home—returning to your roots, I mean."

She thought about what he had written.

"People don't forget, is that what you mean?"

"I guess something like that."

"You think trouble, you'll get trouble. Believe me, I know. I thought you'd been back since . . ."

"Not taking this route—not driving up the heart of the valley middle of the day."

"How'd you get there?"

"Flew in, private plane, middle of the night."

Passing through San Miguel Joanna wanted to stop and visit the mission. John talked her out of it, then became tense when they crossed the Monterey County line.

Joanna, too, was anxious, but preferred not to talk about it—she hoped her daughter wouldn't find their unexpected arrival an unpleasant surprise. They had been at odds, the reason Joanna had sent her off to camp in the first place. Now she was beginning to regret it—the separation seemed to increase the tension in her.

"You really think there will be enough lizards running around to keep the kids occupied?" she said, nervously lighting yet another cigarette.

"You only have to reach down. When I was a kid we found them along the Salinas River, if you knew where to look. They're even thicker in the Carmel Valley along the Carmel River, hotter there. I think it's a natural for a game."

"Texas lizards weren't all that easy to catch," she said.

"Did you try?"

"Sure. I was a game kid."

"The trick for these kids will be to catch the biggest one and the smallest one without losing its tail. You know, how they break off."

The hills were brown and the only water visible in the river was gathered in stagnant pools cupped by river gravel. Normally that wouldn't mean much, because John knew the Salinas River also flows underground and there were times you didn't see water but it was there anyway—you knew by the darkness of the soil and the abundance of the crops.

But now, to the west, dry bursts of wind kicked up loose dirt into dust clouds, dispersing valuable topsoil. What had been grasslands on the far side of the river had given way to more chaparral than John remembered, and the dying leaves of the scattered oaks, coated in dust, were a dirty gray-green. The state was in its third year of drought. Artesian wells had dried up and aquifers pumped empty, and here was John—considered an enemy by many of the growers—coming home, thinking about doing a book about the valley. It now seemed a bad idea.

Just south of San Ardo oil pumps rocked back and forth like feeding dinosaurs. Trucks and workers moved lazily in the rising heat along the flats on the far side of the river. Joanna, her lips parted, a forefinger tapping her teeth, was glad for the diversion—for a minute or two she could forget the adopted daughter who held such anger for her.

"Primal," she thought.

"What?"

"Sorry—thinking aloud. Didn't know I was."

"I do that. Can get you in trouble."

"Tell me," she laughed. "My life story."

After the children's camp they were to meet Elaine, who was flying in. John had called a family handyman and asked him to open up the red Pacific Grove cottage near the coast, air it, stock the outdated refrigerator, weed the yard between the outcroppings of granite and maybe restock the stone pool with fish if raccoons had depleted it.

The deeper they drove into the valley, the more John feared being recognized. He'd grown a goatee and gained weight, but few who'd known him would not recognize him by his luminous eyes. It was in the small towns at stop signs John felt most vulnerable, looking down or away from the driver's window or windshield.

On the highway, he scanned the countryside, taking in as much as he could, storing images. Joanna kept smoking, and whenever John asked for one, she lit and handed him a cigarette with a touch of lipstick on the end, making him smile. They passed through King City, then Greenfield, where a man standing on a wooden walkway stared at the car. John sped up.

"What is it?" Joanna asked.

"Nothing, just paranoia," said John, avoiding a piece of tumbleweed blowing across the road.

"It's a big, pricey car," she said. "Except for the growers, most of these people are dirt poor. You should expect them to stare at it. As a kid in Texas I stared at big cars because I wanted one— who was inside I didn't really give a damn, still don't."

They became quiet.

She looked critically at her hands, then thought—as she often did when she got away from Hollywood—how she hated being frozen in celluloid while aging in the flesh. She'd heard her daughter's friends whisper things about her they wouldn't say about their own mothers, simply because she was a public figure with a famous face.

"You're lucky you're a writer and not an actor," Joanna said.

"What brought that up?"

"Don't know," she lied. "When did you acquire your paranoia?"

"When they put out a contract on me to break my legs."

"That happen?"

"Sure."

"Really?"

"One of many threats long ago. They stay with you."

"That explain not stopping at the mission in San Miguel?"

"Maybe."

They entered Soledad. John looked down at the first stop sign. He knew if he didn't make a full stop he risked getting pulled over. He wanted to say something to Joanna about not looking out the window, being so recognizable. He accelerated the

Oldsmobile smoothly as the road turned back to highway, careful not to speed.

Leaving El Camino Real he skirted his hometown Salinas, taking a narrow back road that looped to the south past a sugar beet processing plant he'd worked at briefly as a young man, finding his way onto the curving highway west to Monterey. As the distance lengthened from Salinas, John grew less tense, Joanna more so.

Reaching Monterey, the Oldsmobile climbed up from the bay and then descended into the lush Carmel Valley.

II

THE CAMP COUNSELORS WOKE THE YOUNGER CHILDREN from their naps while the older kids played board games in the gazebo or on the picnic tables. They were told to not go off on a hike or behind the barn to feed the rabbits in their pens, that an event was scheduled for the afternoon they would not want to miss.

It was Carole's first summer as a counselor. She was tall and freckled with a serene smile that put children and adults at ease. In her mind she didn't differentiate between famous and not-famous people, so John's request by telephone a day earlier to not make their arrival seem anything special made perfect sense to her. She wouldn't have anyway.

Carole was wearing shorts. Like some of the children, her knees were skinned from a morning hike up a steep hillside, but while tending their wounds she had forgotten to see to her own.

Preparing for the visitors, the counselors tacked cloth measuring tape onto one picnic table and put out pitchers of cold lemonade on others. Counselors and children looked up when the Oldsmobile crossed the plank bridge over the Carmel River and started toward them up the dirt road.

"So many kids. I wish we'd bought prizes for them all," Joanna said.

"Do you see Kristen?" asked John.

"Better not to look; she won't like it."

John nodded, pulling the car to a stop, getting out quickly. He opened Joanna's door, waited for her to put out her cigarette and took her by the arm. Smiling—he self-consciously, she radiantly—they strode toward the waiting children and counselors.

Carole introduced John and Joanna, first names only. A girl with blonde bangs moved away to the side but behind a taller boy. She wanted to run off to her cabin, but had waited too long. Joanna didn't look in her daughter's direction.

Carole explained the game John and Joanna had invented. John told them he'd grown up catching lizards on the banks of the Salinas River with his little sister Mary, so perhaps this was a game boys and girls could play together.

"Mary always did better than me," he said.

As the counselors gathered the hats and lariats from the trunk of the Oldsmobile, Joanna told the children, with a slight tremor in her voice, she wished they had something for everyone. For the first time that Kristen could recall, her mother seemed unsure and vulnerable.

"The biggest and smallest lizards in each division win a cowboy hat and a lariat," Carole announced. "You must bring the lizards to the table to be measured. Lizards missing tails will be disqualified in the smallest lizard category and won't have much of a chance in the big lizard category."

"We also have penknives," John added in his rumbling voice.

"I'm not sure about the knives," Carole murmured as she turned to the children.

"I know that some of you have lizards in mason jars in the cabins. These are not eligible for the competition and should be released anyway. How would you like to live in a mason jar? Now off you go!"

Kristen turned and ran into a willow grove by the river, then across the dry riverbed up the opposite bank. She sat down hard, confused. She would not reappear with a lizard, large or small. As she thought this, a large lizard sidled out from a rock and blinked at her. She giggled mockingly. She would not reach down to grab it even if it rolled over to have its stomach tickled. She picked up a pebble and without conviction tossed it in the general direction of the lizard, which blinked back at her but did not budge.

Then she heard Carole's voice.

"Are you going to hurt that beautiful lizard's feelings?" Carole said, looking down at Kristen. "Look at him, he thinks he can win but someone has to enter him in the contest."

"No one told me my mother was coming—I don't want to play," Kristen said. "I thought you were my friend."

"I am—I think you need to see your mother. So does that lizard, don't you think?"

"No."

"Well, it seems to me it does or it'd run away, wouldn't it?"

Kristen looked up at Carole. "Your knees are skinned. Don't they hurt?"

"The pain will go away when I take care of them. It usually does. This lizard seems tame, Kristen. I wonder if it has lived in a mason jar. I think maybe it has. See if you can pick it up."

Kristen thought about it. She bent down with cupped hands and closed them together, scooping up the lizard. It didn't try to escape.

Children were now rushing to the tables with their lizards, which were measured by John and Joanna and the counselors. Then they were released where they had been found. John was laughing, threats and danger far from his mind. He was looking forward to handing out the hats and lariats and, if Carole allowed—which he doubted—the pearl-handled penknives.

Kristen approached cautiously, Carole behind her, a hand on the girl's shoulder. Joanna felt a sense of relief. They both smiled, if hesitantly at first.

"Well, what do you have?" Joanna said as Kristen, looking down, slowly opened her hands.

"That's a handsome one. Let's measure him, shall we?"

The Daughter

T HE WOMAN, LOOKING BACK SOME SEVENTY YEARS, remembered the day her family left this home on the California coast. The white frame house, on a small hill a few blocks above Monterey Bay, was two stories with a steep, green shingle roof. The living room the woman and the couple who owned the house stood talking in had windows of old wavy glass, interior board and batten walls, and a cathedral ceiling of gray tongue-and-groove boards, which had been scavenged, it was said, from a shipwreck a century earlier.

"I remember mornings watching my father walk down the hill to the tide pools from here," the woman said.

"I was four or five, my brother a few years older. We'd watch Dad get smaller and then disappear against the green cypress and the blue of the bay, on those days when it was blue; it was often gray," she said, gazing out to the sea.

"Those were on his lazy days. Most of the time he left when it was still dark before any of us was up. When he left depended on what he wanted to look for in the tide pools. In the afternoons we would sit by the windows waiting for him to come back up the hill," she said, then hesitated before continuing.

"We worried, especially if the sea was rough. Dad could become so lost in his collecting he'd turn his back to the water. He got doused a few times by waves, almost swept out once. So we were always happy and relieved when we saw him safely coming up the hill with his bucket of specimens. Sometimes before he took them to his laboratory he'd show us what he had.

"He'd put the stopper in the kitchen sink, empty the specimens in, and we'd stand on chairs and stare into the sink and he'd tell us what we were looking at, pointing to each little creature or shell or plant and explain its reason for being and what it did and why it was important and fit in. He could get very excited in his quiet way. He used the word 'interdependence' a lot.

"My favorite were the little hermit crabs wearing their tiny protective shells, the way they scampered around and tried to climb up the sides of the sink, falling back then trying again, like a kid trying to climb a tree with slippery bark. They seemed so joyful to me, as if they were racing or playing hide and seek. I know now how frightened the poor things must have been.

"It would irritate Mother, these creatures in her sink. But she knew better than to have dishes in there when Dad came home with a bucket of specimens. When she did it created tension, and that made it uncomfortable for us kids. Sometimes they'd argue, though most of their fights were really about money, because money was always an issue and this was about the time the Great Depression was on its way—so the arguments only got worse."

She lightly touched her dark, graying bangs, remembering, peering first in the direction of the kitchen and then at the man and woman.

"I wonder, do you still have that old white porcelain sink in the kitchen? I imagine it's been replaced, it was so long ago," she said wistfully.

The man and woman who owned the house looked at each other sheepishly. *Yes,* he answered apologetically, the kitchen had been remodeled years ago, the old porcelain sink taken away to . . . to the dump. *We are sorry about that,* the other woman said, looking at her with soft green eyes, *if we had only known. . . .*

"I shouldn't worry about it," the woman smiled.

"I mean, I don't think Dad's sink ranks as historic or anything. Maybe if John had been in this house, had known Dad then and looked at specimens in the sink with Dad, then it might have had more importance, don't you think? Especially if John had written about it. You know, 'And Doc took the specimens home and dumped them in the sink with wash rags and breakfast scrapings. . . .'"

"Of course, Dad would have never done that—put specimens in with washrags—but John took liberties writing about Dad. He had to—he wrote so much about him, but Dad and John met later, a few months after we left here when Mom and Dad were really on the outs. I don't think Dad's friendship with John helped when it came to. . . ."

She was going to say something more but changed her mind.

"I would like to look at the staircase, please. . . ."

The couple glanced at each other again. The woman, who had called several days before and said she had spent the first years of her life in the house and wondered if she could visit, moved to the foot of the stairs and studied the staircase as the couple watched. There wasn't much to the staircase; it was rather utilitarian with a plain banister. It had five broad steps, then took a turn to the right and continued up to a balcony, which led to two bedrooms.

"Well, I feel better now," she said thoughtfully.

"Better?" the woman with green eyes said.

"The day we moved out, Mother put Auntie in charge of me so I wouldn't get in the way. It was a terrible day. We were all unhappy. Dad was quiet—even for him—and I remember Mom watching him, while a few friends moved our furniture out to a truck. My brother and I knew Mom and Dad were angry and unhappy and that our lives as we knew them were probably coming to an end. Auntie knew it too and pulled me over here by the staircase so I would be out of the way. My brother was sent outside—out there. I wasn't old enough to be trusted without supervision, especially outside."

She looked out the windows at the front yard, her sad eyes lingering as if she could see her brother again, then back at the staircase.

"You see, I got into a lot of trouble as a kid. You'll laugh. For some reason I thought I could fly back then. I really did. Any time I was anxious, I wanted to fly. Maybe I wanted to fly away. I jumped off walls and over gutters and cats and puddles when it rained. I loved it when it rained and there were puddles. I really felt I could take wing. I was probably trying to get Dad's attention; I already had Mom's but I exasperated her and I knew it. I wanted Dad to pay as much attention to me as he did to his hermit crabs. I wanted him to understand his children were also interdependent, just like his specimens.

"That moving day, Mom and Dad were standing right there, working at a table, wrapping things in paper—dishes and things to be put in boxes—but not saying anything to each other. That made me really anxious. I knew Dad wished he could just leave the packing to the others, just walk out and go down to the tide pools and search for creatures, because that's what he always did when he wanted to get away—that or go to a bar and have a few beers—and of course Mom knew that. I thought he might just walk out any second and Mom would be so upset, so hurt.

"It frightened me, so I told Auntie to hold her arms out and I climbed up the stairs and turned and yelled and jumped into her arms. I did it again and again. Dad looked over once, Mom not at all. I pretended I was having fun but I was wretched, my stomach in knots. I wanted to hurt myself. I hurt Auntie instead—she fell back and bumped against the window right there and I could tell she was in pain. But she didn't stop me from jumping, she seemed to know I needed to do it. Auntie understood me and loved me, and I was a selfish child."

She sighed.

"I've always felt guilty for what I put her through that day. You see, I remembered the staircase having more steps to the turn, so I feel better now seeing it's not so high as I remembered—and I hope I went up only a few steps—though I still made it very difficult for Auntie . . .

"Isn't that odd, thinking I could fly? Who can explain a child's mind? I guess I had a lot of anxiety about my parents because I kept trying to fly. Then one day, after they separated, I jumped off the stairs of Dad's laboratory on the waterfront, but this time Auntie wasn't there to catch me and I finally managed to hurt myself—I broke both my arms on the concrete sidewalk. I was in casts for the longest time. So that cured me forever of thinking I could fly . . . but I still get anxious, of course . . . I mean you never really lose that . . . once you learn you can't fly. . . ."

Dora and Flora

DORA AND FLORA HAD IN COMMON BEING OF THE SAME species and general place of birth, but that was about all. Dora was stuffy and stiff, expression glazed and artificial. Flora was svelte and sensual, quick and dangerous with alive, darting eyes.

Dora would end up on a British warship, much loved of men, often patted on the head for luck, especially in times of danger. Flora would make her home in a London zoo, beloved of men, women and children, not to be patted under any circumstance.

A meeting on a summer eve in 1959 would lead to the final destination of the two big cats. An American writer named John entertained a Royal Navy lieutenant named Wellesley at the writer's rented Somerset cottage. The two men sat enjoying a drink called scrumpy, made from small withered apples, or scrimps which, when fermented, produce a powerful alcoholic cider.

The lieutenant served aboard the *H.M.S. Puma*, one of several anti-aircraft vessels named for big cats. He found it lamentable, he told his host after a second scrumpy, that the *Puma* was the only frigate without a wardroom mascot—in each case a mounted head of the big cat the vessel was named for.

"Why," John said, "I don't know if you're aware of it, but I come from Monterey County in California, and pumas abound in our mountains and valleys. Wouldn't you rather have a whole puma body than just a head? And wouldn't you rather have the puma alive than stuffed?"

Wellesley said he didn't think a vessel involved in battle or maneuvers could manage a live puma, even in a cage. But a puma stuffed and bolted down would certainly give his ship bragging rights.

The next day, nursing a hangover, John wrote a letter to his friend Jimmy, a Monterey newspaperman, explaining the situation. Jimmy thought a stuffed puma going to a friendly navy a grand idea, and wrote a newspaper story about it. Readers were asked to be on the lookout for a stuffed puma.

While response was enthusiastic, the nearest anyone came was a female puma head and skin, used as a rug in the lobby of a Salinas hotel. The hotel donated it and readers paid for it to be groomed, stuffed and mounted on a redwood base. Writing about this and realizing the description "stuffed puma" lacked charm, Jimmy named the mounted feline Dora, intentionally echoing the name of a female character—Flora—immortalized by John in one of his books.

Excited, John arranged to have Dora flown to England and delivered to the *H.M.S. Puma*. With help Jimmy loaded Dora into his station wagon and drove her to the San Francisco airport where Dora was photographed with two smiling Pan-American stewardesses before being flown over the Polar Cap.

More press followed in England, including a photograph appearing in newspapers throughout the British Isles of John and Royal Navy sailors patting Dora's head and body. This led to a zoo director contacting John, which led to more scrumpies in Somerset, which led to a request by the zoo director, which led to John writing Jimmy again.

John wanted Jimmy to get down to Big Sur and find a *live* puma for a British zoo. Jimmy knew this would be difficult in such a wild land. A novelist once wrote that either you adapted to Big Sur or it would reject you and send you to a kind of purgatory, to which a poet added that hardened inhabitants spurned the sun and drank fog like rain.

Jimmy understood both men. He recalled once scrambling up a hill on a misty morning pursuing a story on runaways. Looking up, he saw half naked young men and women staring down at him. He rubbed his eyes. When he opened them again they had vanished into the fog and brush. If *they* could disappear in an instant, what were his chances of finding a puma? And what would he do with it if he did?

So Jimmy let it be known he needed expert help. He was told a tracker-trapper named Mathis lived deep in the mountains, in a cabin inaccessible by car and without a phone. "You may have to track *him*," he was warned. "He's hard to find because he doesn't want to be found."

Jimmy drove down the coast. North of the village he pulled over and asked a man walking on the shoulder of the road if he knew of a trapper named Mathis. "Trapper? Hell, I'm from Cleveland," the man said. "I'm looking for my son. Tall, long brown hair, plays the guitar badly. If you see him, tell him his mother cries every day."

The villagers, however, did know Mathis—he hiked out of the mountains now and then to purchase supplies and drink beer, they said, but no telling when. Jimmy would have to wait around or trek in to find him. Discouraged, Jimmy had a beer at a place called Nepenthe on a hill by the Pacific Ocean with a view of the mountains to the east. Jimmy was on his second beer when a waitress yelled to the bartender:

"Look—here comes Mathis! Do we have enough beer?"

"Where?" asked Jimmy.

Peering through the bar's telescope, the waitress replied, "He's a few ridges over."

She let Jimmy have a look. He made out a big bearded man with a walking staff making his way gingerly down a mountain.

"When will he get here?"

"It's late and he has a limp," said the waitress. "He'll camp tonight and show up tomorrow—mid morning, I'd guess."

"I need to talk to him."

"Then stay where you are. He comes here for his first round of beers."

So Jimmy came back the next day and waited until Mathis came through the door and began downing beers. Mathis gave the waitresses and bartender the latest backcountry news, which included hippies moving into a nearby canyon, disturbing the peace.

"One play a guitar?" Jimmy said.

Mathis glanced at Jimmy with mild curiosity and grunted, "Badly—and loud, too."

"He's from Cleveland. If I see his father I'll tell him."

"Please do. He should go home and take lessons."

Mathis became quiet, scratching his thick red beard. Jimmy cleared his throat and broached the subject of trapping a puma for a British zoo.

"What's England done for me?" Mathis asked, shifting uncomfortably on his bar stool while gazing yearningly at the hills.

"We were allies in World War II," explained Jimmy.

"I only remember the first one—which is why I limp and live back there," he said, gesturing to the hills.

Then he thought a while over a few more beers.

"I'll tell you what—you say a puma would have a good life in that English zoo? Treated well, fed well, given good care? You know that sure?"

"John said it would, and I believe John."

Mathis thought, had another beer, then thought some more.

"The puma population's lower than when . . . what's your name anyway?"

"Jimmy."

"Well, Jimmy, puma population's low and I don't want to deplete it more. But there's this exception . . . I have this young female mountain lion named Flora—"

"*Flora?*"

"Yes, I've always liked the name."

"*Flora!*"

"Yes—*Flora!* What I was trying to say—Flora's back in the mountains, hanging out around my place. Found her as a cub, mother'd been run over on the highway. She's no good hunting anything bigger'n a squirrel, thinks grizzlies are playthings, sleeps on my roof, can't stay away from chickens. Doesn't have much sense, missing a mother's wisdom. I worry something happens to me, what happens to Flora? . . . Anyway, like to think she'd be safe . . . even if it has to be a zoo."

So they talked some more and a deal was struck. Jimmy wrote John who, again excited, arranged for Flora, once brought in, to be flown from San Francisco to London. Mathis wasn't sure when he'd get back to the village because sometimes Flora took it in her head to roam, requiring Mathis to wait for the young puma to make her way back, usually when she was hungry.

Weeks later a waitress at Nepenthe spotted Mathis and Flora coming over the hills, the lean puma tugging on a leash, Mathis leaning on his staff. They arrived the next day to meet Jimmy, who'd borrowed a pickup truck with a cage. Mathis said they'd spent the night under the stars and he woke with Flora's whiskered chin on his chest. The trapper's eyes were damp, red as his beard.

Mathis guided the nervous Flora onto the truck bed and into the cage. He reached through the bars and rubbed behind the moaning puma's ears, her nose in the air, tears running down his cheeks into his beard.

He looked at the hills, considering, then abruptly turned and climbed the hill to the Nepenthe bar, Flora yowling after him. She yowled most of the way to the airport, looking to the hills to the east, alarming other motorists.

Jimmy was saddened to pass a suddenly silent Flora on to Pan American. He told himself it was for the best, imagining Flora in her new home in England as John and all Britain toasted her with scrumpies. Jimmy wrote in the paper the next day that Flora was thought to be the first live puma to fly the Polar Cap.

Mathis, some said, did not come out of the hills again. When asked about the trapper, Jimmy would say, "He knew something."

A Bar in Athens

IT WAS A DANGEROUS TIME IN ATHENS WITH A MILITARY coup in the works and a king in peril, but still the American carrier sailors were allowed shore leave while warned to lay off political talk, especially anything concerning Greece. The crew of the carrier had just served three months "on the line" off the coast of Vietnam, and relaxing was in order.

Jackie, a petty officer third-class, blue-eyed with short-cropped blond hair, was not interested in politics anyway, nor visiting the Acropolis or any other famous attraction. A loner by nature, he separated from the others, got a room in a small hotel and found a waterfront bar hard by a pier, a dark, smoke-filled place where, when the conversation quieted, one could hear lapping water. Jackie had lived two years with that sound and found it comforting, had become dependent on it. Sometimes he dreamed he was trapped inland, and it felt suffocating and claustrophobic to him.

In Navy dress whites, he found a seat at the plank bar, placing his hat on it, and ordered a beer. To his right, an empty stool between them, sat a large older man in a dark tee shirt and brown corduroy sport coat. On the other side of the large man was someone as young as Jackie—wearing a raincoat despite there being no hint of rain, and glasses with dark rims. He was writing in a notebook. The large man looked over at Jackie and smiled and said in a gravelly voice that immediately identified him as an American, "The Navy has landed, I saw your carrier, welcome, son," and reached over with a pack of cigarettes, giving it a tilt and a shake so a few cigarettes slid forward in the pack. Jackie said thank you but declined.

The older man, dragging deeply on his cigarette and sipping clear liquor from a glass which seemed dainty in his large hand, stared straight ahead at shelves of liquor and wine bottles and a rusty anchor bolted to the wall. Now and then he said something in his rumbling low voice and the younger man to his right would make a note, the large man watching him and nodding. Jackie thought the older man's nose looked to have been broken a time or two, that perhaps he had been a boxer in his youth. He wore a graying goatee and his receding hair was messily pushed back as if with his hand rather than a brush or a comb. When one cigarette went out, he lit another. The bartender, whom the regulars called out to as Nikos, refilled the large man's glass then brought Jackie another beer—paid for by "the big man here," said Nikos.

Jackie thanked the big man for a second time and the big man, not looking at him, gestured and smiled, and rumbled something else—Jackie thought he heard the word Vietnam, but then Vietnam was often on his mind—which the young man in the raincoat and dark-rimmed glasses, who was swigging his drinks, apparently wrote down.

The big man became melancholy and made no effort to hide it, in fact might have been dramatizing it, Jackie thought. He rubbed his eyes, ignoring something the young man in the raincoat said to him. The young man seemed resigned, closed his notebook and set it on the bar and stared at his drink.

Jackie wondered at the relationship of the two men but then picked up the conversation of several other men at a table behind him. They were speaking Greek. Maybe he was imaging it, but he thought the conversation tense and twice he heard the name Konstantinos in whispered voices. Jackie knew enough about Greece to know that the king carried that name.

He also felt someone at the table was talking about him. He turned slightly and saw one of the men looking at him. The man, wearing a military uniform, met Jackie's eyes and smiled easily, charmingly. Jackie turned back to the bar and wondered if he might have picked a better place. But then maybe any bar was a bad idea in these times, perhaps visiting the Acropolis was a better one. So he found himself saying half to himself and half to the older man—the big man—but not looking at him, "You know, I'd sure like to be out in the open countryside right about now, riding a motorcycle down some lonesome highway."

The big man turned to Jackie, inspecting him closely for the first time with strangely luminous blue eyes. "You know, that's not a bad idea, I was roughly thinking something like that myself." Jackie's remark seemed to have changed his mood and he turned his whole body toward Jackie, glass in one hand, cigarette in the other, waited a moment, then said, "Tell me, son, if you could do that—just take off like you said—where would you ride?"

Jackie thought about it. "I'd ride across the country—the United States, I mean," he said, noticing the young man in the dark-rimmed glasses opening his notebook again.

"Well, it's good to know your country, and that's a fine way to do it. What would you ride?"

"I said a motorcycle—I think a Triumph maybe. I'd want the open air."

"A Triumph! So you like British bikes? So do I." He looked at the young man to his right who was writing again and said, "Please." The young man in the black-rimmed glasses sighed and closed his notebook.

"You were saying?" the older man said.

"Well, I bought a Triumph in England last year," Jackie boasted.

"You can afford a Triumph on a petty officer's pay?"

"I'm making payments. It will be waiting for me in New York when I'm discharged. Hopefully not paid off."

"Why do you say that?"

"Payments are three years. I want to be back in civvies before three years are up. Then I'll take that trip across the country."

"Trips take you, or so I've found in my experience."

"That's okay with me," Jackie said amiably. "Just so it's me out there on the road. I'd rent a garage and tune and polish it first, before leaving I mean."

"Would you?"

"Yes, I'd shine it up. I do that on the carrier."

"Do you?" The big man was warming up to him. "How do you mean?"

"Well, I polish the jets. I shine them up."

"That's what you do?"

Jackie thought for a moment, then said, "Well, I do more. I guess a lot more, but I don't like talking about it."

"Very well, son. You just enjoy your beer," and the big man turned and looked at the wall, becoming melancholy again. Jackie began feeling guilty.

Finally he said, "Well, I'm what you call a plane captain. I'm in charge of several jets."

"Preparation and all?" said the big man.

"Yeah, making sure it's ready for combat, ready to go. It can be pretty nerve-wracking, maybe that's why I don't like talking about it."

"I understand, no need, I understand."

"But I don't mind telling you," he said, wondering why that was and why he was saying it. "You see, and I don't want you to take this wrong, but when I'm working on a plane, checking instruments and fuel levels and cleaning it up, I imagine . . . I imagine I'm back in the States getting my car ready for a hot date."

"Good idea. What kind of car?"

"I imagine a Jaguar XKE. White."

"English again."

"I hadn't thought of that."

The big man grinned. "You are some boy," he said.

"Well, if a pilot walks in, don't tell him what I just said. I don't think he would want to know his F-111 is really a Jaguar that can't take off."

"It's strictly between us."

Jackie glanced at the young man in the dark-rimmed glasses taking notes again. When the big man looked at him and said, "Please," the other man put his pen down and lifted his glass and took a drink. "Writing drives some men to drink. Not writing does it to Jim."

"Anyway, it's important work. When I strap the pilot in, everything better damn well be ready, you know?"

"I think I do."

"So after I make sure she's roadworthy, my new Triumph, I take off across the country and end up in California—so coast to coast, ocean to ocean. I'd finish it on one of those curving

canyon roads with the smell of eucalyptus, then coming out
above the Pacific, breathing in the sea."

The older man smiled. "I know the topography well," he said.
"And the scent of eucalyptus mixed with sea air—I know that,
too. I wish I was younger and taking that trip with you. I did it
once, a few years ago, but not on a motorbike."

They talked for several hours—the older man never giving his
name and Jackie not asking. When they said goodnight, Jackie
left the bar first, a little drunk. The men who had been seated
at the table behind him had already gone. But Jackie was still
nervous about them and kept an eye out as he made his way
carefully through the dark streets back toward his hotel.

Men were gathered on corners, in uniform and civvies, smoking and speaking in low voices, and to Jackie there seemed suspicion and menace everywhere. His room seemed a haven. He
went to sleep thinking of the older man, wondering about him
and the young note-taker.

Jackie arrived at the bar a little later the next night. He was
relieved the men in uniform were not there, disappointed the big
man and the note-taker were absent. He took the same stool at
the bar he had the previous night.

Then the Greek military man, the one Jackie was sure had
been talking about him the night before, came in, catching
Jackie's eye, tipping his hat, smiling charmingly. Jackie gestured
vaguely, his heart racing—the timing seemed too coincidental.
The man sat at the same table and in a few minutes he was
joined by another man, also in uniform. Jackie shifted uncomfortably on his stool; he did not like having his back to people he
felt were watching him.

Anyway, he couldn't understand the interest in someone like
himself, a petty officer whatever his country. Jackie was proud of

knowing nothing about operations until he was given orders, and wanted to keep it that way. Nikos brought him a beer and said in a whisper, "Don't worry. They're here to watch the big man."

"The big man?"

"The big man who bought you all those beers to make you drunk last night." Nikos gestured to where the man had been sitting.

"Why would they want to watch him?"

"I don't know, but they do. They have done it three nights in a row."

"Does he know?" Jackie said.

"I think so. But I think he does not care—he keeps coming back. It will make four nights tonight."

"Do you think he will be back again?"

"I think so. There, you see? He's here now with his friend with the notebook." Nikos smiled and moved off.

The big man and the younger man in the raincoat had just entered. The big man smiled at Jackie, then took the stool he had occupied the night before, so again there was an empty stool between them. The young man in the raincoat sat to his right as before, opened his notebook and wiped raindrops off his heavy black-rimmed glasses.

"I told you it would rain," he said.

"You told me three days ago. You should be a weatherman," the big man laughed, then looked at Jackie.

"We looked out at your carrier again today, quite a boat. Someone told me she just came from Vietnam."

Nikos delivered a small glass of clear liquor to the big man and an amber-colored liquor in a larger glass to the young man in the raincoat.

"Thank you, Nikos," the big man rumbled.

"We arrived back in the Mediterranean a few weeks ago," said Jackie.

"I was thinking about what you said last night. You are a bright young man. You think for yourself and you have imagination. What do you read?"

"Not much of anything. I'm a bad student; that's why I'm in the Navy. I know who Shakespeare was and who Longfellow was and I guess that's about it."

The big man smiled. "I knew I liked you. You reminded me of George last night and you still do."

"George?"

"A policeman in Monterey, in California. A motorcycle cop. Like you, very frank, very to the point. His uniform was blue with high boots, you know."

"He ever give you a ticket?"

"Once, and laughed while he wrote it."

"Did you laugh?"

"Sure—once I got over his effrontery it was pretty damn funny. But to be honest, I guess that was a few days later."

"We have dress blues, but too hot now. I wouldn't mind being a motorcycle cop someday, maybe when I get out," said Jackie.

"As I say, there are similarities, you and George," said the older man. "George isn't much of a reader either. We were good friends."

"Because he didn't read much?"

"Could be. I'm closer to him than to a lot of people I know who read a lot, but many of them are reading bad stuff so maybe that doesn't count as reading."

Then he became quiet again, turning his gaze to the bottles of liquor and the anchor attached to the wall. Jackie cleared his throat. The big man thought about George the motorcycle cop and the times they spent talking nonsense and he wished he could go back to that time. He remembered George always in uniform, first as a scout and then as a football player and then as a motorcycle cop. And so, he realized suddenly, he would probably always remember Jackie in his dress whites, and then, with a sense of dread, he thought he would remember his own sons Thom and John only in military uniforms. The idea frightened him.

"What are your pilots like?" he asked quickly, not looking at Jackie.

"Nice guys, couple big heads, but you have to be to do what they do. Ran into one today. He does read, lot smarter than me, named Reggie. Went to one of those Eastern schools."

"Reggie's on leave too?"

"Sure. He was sightseeing, had a guidebook, heading for a museum. Asked me along."

"You didn't go?"

Jackie shook his head.

"Museums make me feel dumb sometimes. I might bring Reggie by to meet you tomorrow night. I told him about you and Jim."

"That would be nice, if we're here, I don't know," he said, glancing over his shoulder at the two military men at the table.

The big man seemed troubled, then said slowly, "What do you think of the war, Jackie?"

"I don't think about it much, but when I do, I guess not much."

"I see," the big man said.

"I'll tell you what I do about that: I pretend I'm fighting for my family and that's it, though I know the Vietcong are no threat to them, of course. But there are times I need some kind of motivation, something to keep me going, you know?"

"Sure, I guess."

"I especially imagine I'm fighting for my kid sister Mary. I don't want anything hurting her. She's been hurt enough."

The big man stared at Jackie. "You know, I had a kid sister named Mary."

"Yeah?"

"Yeah. She died." The big man thought of his sister. "She was a tomboy, got into a lot of trouble. I felt pretty protective of her when we were growing up, just like you do for your sister. I always did."

"Well, we have something in common."

"I knew that from the beginning. It was a feeling."

"What did your sister Mary look like when she was a kid?"

The big man laughed.

"Hard to tell—she was so dirty all the time, drove Mother crazy. Would go through two or three pair of coveralls a summer. But when you got the dirt off, Mary was pretty, very pretty. But mainly, she was spirited—you couldn't discourage Mary, no matter what you did, and believe me I tested her plenty. And your little sister?"

"Well, that's the thing . . . ," Jackie said, hesitating. "She's pretty, too, but has a . . . what you might call a facial disfigurement. . . ."

"I'm sorry."

Jackie looked into his beer glass. "Yeah, poor kid—it's pretty tough for her if you know what I mean. . . ."

The big man waited for a moment. "There are operations."

"Yeah. We'll get it fixed. Mom and Dad will see to that."

"Good."

"But it's been difficult for her, a little kid like that. The thing is, she has guts—she refuses to hide away, to hide in shadow. So that's who I imagine I'm fighting for—for my kid sister."

"Damn good idea."

"I think about her when I'm shining up those jets."

"Not just the Jaguar?"

"No, not just the Jaguar."

"Nikos," the big man said, gesturing, and Nikos brought drinks all around.

The big man hoisted his glass. "To kid sisters," he said softly.

Around midnight the young man in the black-rimmed glasses pitched forward, his head thudding onto the bar. The big man looked at him and said, "Jim's from Berkeley. He can handle pot but not booze—kids these days! If he'd smoked pot here in Athens, he'd never get out of the country."

He gestured in the direction of the two men in uniform behind them. "But there's no law against this. We'll let him rest. He'll be okay in an hour or two. He wants to be a playwright."

Jackie came into the bar the next night with the pilot Reggie. There had been disturbances in the streets; cautiously detouring around them, they were later than Jackie wanted to be. The big man was there with the note-taker, who had a bruise on the right side of his face. He had closed his notebook and was buttoning his raincoat when Jackie and Reggie walked in. The big man was gathering his cigarettes and matches, and had one foot on a stool rung and the other on the floor while finishing his drink.

He smiled. "Hello, Jackie."

Jackie introduced Reggie, and the big man, giving no name, shook Reggie's hand and thanked him for his service. At a nearby table the two men in military uniforms watched.

"You're leaving?" Jackie asked.

"Yes," said the big man. "We have an early morning flight. We need to get out while we can—the city's on edge."

"I'll say," said Reggie. "We just saw some of it."

"Nikos," the big man said, and put money on the plank bar. "For their drinks, you get what's left. Thank you, my friend."

The two Greek military men stood and the one who smiled at Jackie the first night looked at the big man and said casually in English: "We're not so bad, are we, sir? Be nice to our country if you write about her."

"She is a wonderful country. I hope she finds peace."

"As do we, but there's work to be done, and can it be done peacefully? I think not."

He tipped his hat and followed his companion out the door.

The big man waited then took Jackie's hand. "It's been a pleasure. You've reminded me of my sons and I thank you for that. I'll think about you riding across the country on your Triumph motorcycle. In two years, you said?"

"I hope."

"Good."

Then he looked away and said, "Jim," took his friend by the arm and, his head down, his face flushed, ushered him quickly out the door without looking back.

Jackie and Reggie sat at the plank bar.

"I know what he drinks. What will you have?" Nikos said.

Reggie asked for a beer then turned to Jackie, puzzled. "You don't follow the scuttlebutt much, do you, Jackie?"

Jackie shook his head. "You know me."

"Well, that big guy, he's a writer. If my information is correct, he's either returning from or on his way to Vietnam to make an assessment for the president on the level of morale."

Jackie thought about that as Reggie took a swig of his beer.

Jackie said, "We both have kid sisters named Mary."

On Stolen Time

I

EXHAUSTED, PAUL COMES HOME TO HIS COTTAGE AND wife. It's close to midnight and he's just led a men's support group for a disease that afflicts him, too. He undresses quietly, stands silently and considers sleeping on the sofa. He's afraid of startling Pat with one of his nightmares, thrashing about, crying out, body shaking and soaked in perspiration, bad for him, worse for her.

But he needs her warmth. He slips into bed and moves close to her. He thinks, decides. In the morning he will look for old books, anything related to writing. He needs that, too. The session tonight was particularly difficult and his only relief is in the search for literature. He is a collector.

He plans for tomorrow. Maybe a stop at the Goodwill on the off chance he might beat one of the dealers to a find. Odds slight because one or two of the dealers may have an arrangement with the store manager, but now and then something interesting makes it through—

—Paul finds a volume of Saroyan short stories autographed to the early Wimbledon champ Helen Wills Moody and a man named Aidan Roark. Paul's research reveals that Roark was an

Irish film actor and polo star and Helen's first husband. Did they meet at Wimbledon? The book is now part of his collection.

—Or Paul glances at the wall of leaning paintings and prints and a yellowed acid-burned Rembrandt etching of the master himself looks out at him with melancholy eyes. To Paul, also melancholy, no one looks into himself like Rembrandt and he trembles when he takes it in his hands. After conservation it now hangs on his study wall.

Then before or after Goodwill he'll work his way through the dealers, trading stories, gossiping, seeing what old books are new in inventory, hoping for something unique, elusive—something to enrich his collection.

He'll see Ron, grinning, in his bookshop, the space a terrible choice with floor-to-ceiling windows that let the sun flood in if blinds aren't pulled, fading the spines of the books, many of them first editions. Ron is brilliant but at loose ends, doesn't know where to find a particular valuable book on his shelves when someone asks after it, blames thieves then finds the book, often after the client leaves, deal shot but then another collector always comes along.

Or Richard, sitting on a bench outside his shop, smoking cigarettes inserted into a tortoise shell water-filter holder. Richard rising quickly, smiling shyly and nodding and looking down and holding the door for Paul while freeing and snubbing out his cigarette on the sidewalk. Richard gets along with books, feels at home with them.

There are six or seven shops, the names changing as dealers die or take ill at their work, people seldom retiring from a passion, their places taken by others recklessly giving up real jobs. As he moves from shop to shop, Paul will see other collectors with a passion for the written word and the feel and smell of books and letters and their usually poor relations, ephemera. Maybe he'll go for coffee with another collector to top off the morning.

Then he stops thinking about the morning. The experience of the past evening counseling ill men forces its way into his head uninvited. Men discussing how they're holding up, releasing held-in emotions, what research is hopeful and may save them—and what is promising but, if it comes, will come too late and they know it.

A new man showed up late, name's Ralph, said he didn't see the value of a support group when he'd die soon anyway, but he promised his wife and his daughters he'd give it a try, so here he was, but only for them, only to satisfy his family.

Paul had seen many Ralphs over the years, usually prophetic about how long they have to live. Paul works with them but doesn't want them bringing others down, so only so much time and patience, and this night less than usual, for he had fears of his own, recent bouts of a sudden oncoming dizziness he has dreaded, didn't want to think about. Ralph felt Paul's reluctance, then Ralph left the session, slipped out early, and Paul realized—realizes—he had/has done his job poorly this night.

Paul was a financial consultant for a bank in San Francisco when the doctor gave him five years to live, "six at the outside," which made Paul consider how long "the inside" might be. So he took early retirement and moved down the coast with Pat to the red cottage they now call home, and founded the support group. No longer working, he indulged his passion for books, living those more-or-less-promised five years, then surpassed the "outside"—then ten, fifteen and twenty years, shocking not only the doctors but himself.

"I'm a thief. I am living on stolen time," he announces. "I last because I have a wonderful wife and I do what I love. I have no complaints."

II

LIGHTHOUSE AVENUE IN NEW MONTEREY IS A HEAVY-traffic, stop-and-start boulevard of bars, fifteen-dollar haircuts, Mexican, Italian and Asian restaurants, furniture stores and a succession of used and rare bookshops. Be warned: it's hard to spot any particular business while driving, because there are always cars on your tail and to slow down is to court a rear-ender.

Paul makes it through the night without disturbing Pat, who is to give a tour at the Carmel Mission this morning. Paul leaves first, on the road in his little white pickup. The bookshops are tucked into odd, tight spaces: next to a key shop, between an art supply store and a British pub, backing onto the waterfront, catty-corner from a Lebanese takeout that bakes its own flatbread, all on Lighthouse. Why the book dealers gather in this district is not known, but rent is low and most dealers operate on a shoestring.

And there's a mystical belief that the strip was destined for bookshops since Steinbeck made the trip down Lighthouse frequenting bars now vanished. In San Francisco, Paul collected Fitzgerald, Cather and Hemingway. Now Steinbeck is a priority; he lived here, material pops up, and Paul loves his compassion, calls it up when his own is tested by difficult times with his support group.

He visits first Richard's Books and Things, but this morning no Richard sitting on a bench smoking filter-tip cigarettes in a tortoise shell holder. A man stands reading a note posted on the door. Paul approaches. The note reads the shop is temporarily closed, Richard is in the hospital. Paul guesses lung cancer. It seemed inevitable.

The man standing at the door says he has done business with Richard, likes him, found a coveted Ambrose Bierce first edition through him. His name's Leon, drove down from Palo Alto.

Crisp, expensive clothing: buffed brown loafers, gray cashmere rolled-collar jacket, beige wool slacks with a slight break an inch above the cuffs. Leon's a particular collector type—well to do, easily able to afford the most expensive signed first editions. Paul's another type, feels tacky in his jeans and coffee-stained windbreaker.

They talk of their collections. Leon says his grown children have no interest in his and he's leaving it to a university, accompanied by a generous endowment with his name on it.

Paul's thoughts run along the same line, though an endowment's out of the question; his money will see Pat through her final years. But he agrees with Leon that collecting is a creative endeavor. Paul thinks of himself as a saver of words, not a writer or a critic, but the kind of person—and he includes Leon—literature needs.

"Collectors are never given enough credit," Leon says operatically. "We are trustees of whatever we collect, be it literature or art or cultural icons as trivial as bottle caps. If you ask me, that's what I think."

Paul smiles at the idea of bottle caps as cultural icons, yet can't argue with it. Leon is suddenly restless, looks at the road, his watch, fishes for his keys and says goodbye, pulls away in a burgundy car twice the size and many times the value of Paul's pickup.

Paul knows Leon's off to the other shops, would normally feel competitive someone's beating him to treasures. But this morning he sits back on Richard's bench wondering if Richard will ever return to reopen his shop, or if he will die in the hospital where Paul has seen men from his group pass away over the years, always feeling he should be there for them.

Richard has no children; if he dies his inventory will likely be wholesaled to cover debts and the place closed, perhaps boarded up, unless another dealer takes the lease or the building is torn down. Paul has a feeling he will not see Richard again, just as he will not see Ralph, the man who came to the support group late and left early.

He feels dizzy, lies to himself it's the sun, makes his way to his truck, drives up Lighthouse passing Goodwill and bookshops. He dimly realizes what he is up to—leapfrogging Leon. He'll hit Ron's, the last of the string of bookshops on the thoroughfare before New Monterey becomes Pacific Grove. He'll beat Leon to one place, at least.

He comes in through the sliding glass door behind Ron, who is paging through an old book. Ron looks up, greets Paul with his shy smile. Ron came out from Michigan decades ago, began his business in the living room of his apartment a few blocks up the steep hill from Lighthouse, then found this tight little two-level space with tattered carpet and too much sunlight. Without a car or any interest in owning one, Ron walks to work and the stores and libraries, and to Doctors on Duty when he is ill, but it must be very.

In his early years Ron took college entrance exams for friends in Michigan and at nineteen flew to Paris to be Hemingway. When he returned to Detroit he taught autistic children and loved it and became a computer guru and helped companies. But he hated the hours and felt something was missing so traveled to Los Angeles to be Paul Newman. Between walk-ons as an extra he cut and laid linoleum in Southern California kitchens and hall entrances.

With sore knees he made his way north to the Monterey Peninsula where he remembered he loved reading and purchased a book collection for four dollars per book and set up shop, pricing and selling the books for eight dollars each. They went quickly, some first editions worth hundreds. Ron laughed and educated himself.

Ron's shy but inquisitive personality worked with collectors and he felt he belonged. If a collector was tapped or couldn't quite afford an edition, Ron would accommodate him however he could. If an individual played him for what he knew but gave nothing in return, Ron cut him off. Otherwise he was happy making a living doing what he loved, and the engaging grin seldom left his face.

"Do you have something for me?" Paul says.

"Do I ever have something for you!" Ron replies, excited, asking Paul to guess then stands there, waiting, grinning. Paul normally enjoys Ron's games, playing them out, does not today, knows Leon is on his way, could walk in any minute.

He smiles but there it is again, the dizziness, yet, more urgently he wants to know what the something is that Ron has acquired— and he wants to know before Leon pulls up in his big burgundy car and walks through the door in his fine clothes. So he pleads and Ron laughs and gives in, pointing to the shelves on the second level.

"Third shelf center—a conflicted letter from John to his first wife Carol. Heavy, emotional, discusses *Mice*, I tell you the scholars will love it. Major find! In a red folder."

This excites Paul, something important for his collection, perhaps the crowning piece he desires, a newly discovered Steinbeck letter. He climbs the few steps to the upper level he has taken hundreds of times and reaches for the red folder with his right hand but comes up short and falls forward, landing heavily face down. He remains still, then feels Ron's powerful hands grab each side of his chest and pull him up to a sitting position as if he were a limp doll.

The falls have begun. He realizes now he's coming to the end. He thinks of Richard and Ralph, and wonders who among the three of them will die first, and that makes him smile, and in that smile Ron misreads him, finds encouragement and asks, coming from a distance, "Feeling better, Paul?"

Paul lies the falls are expected and nothing to worry about. He holds out both hands and Ron helps him to his feet, steadies him, fetches the red folder with the letter and puts it carefully in his right hand, the hand he reached out with, gives it a pat, Ron does.

"Look it over and let me know what you think. Yours if we can agree on the price. I warn you, Paul, I paid a lot, it won't be cheap," but says it with a smile, then looking at Paul closely asks, "Should you drive? Do you want me to call Pat?"

Paul shakes his head then makes his way carefully out of the shop and to his white pickup. He's a little panicky. A high price for the letter wouldn't deter Leon. As he pulls away he sees Leon in his cashmere rolled-collar jacket coming up the sidewalk, entering Ron's shop. He pats the red folder on the seat by him—if he'd been just a few minutes later getting to Ron's it would not be his. For a while he forgets the fall.

When he gets home Pat's still gone, giving the tour at the Carmel Mission, perhaps having lunch now with other docents. Good, she will not see him this way. He centers the folder on his desk. He puts his fingers to his lips and then, gently, to the folder.

Paul has something to eat then falls into a deep sleep. He will read the letter when he wakes, then take his time showing it to Pat before formally placing it in his collection, which he has arranged chronologically. He knows it's probably his last acquisition, but a good one. He has no complaints.

The Gaunt Visitor

H E WAS LEANING OVER HIS DESK, WRITING, PENCIL ON yellow legal pad, occasionally glancing at the whispering tape recorder, finished an entry and picked up the pad, and read in the direction of the recorder in his deep voice, "There was a gap in the hills, dark, a place he found menacing, a place he had every intention of not entering."

"Who're you talking to?"

He looked up. The speaker stood before the dark window; behind him through the open blinds the lights of a city blinked in the night.

"Oh, it's you, it's been a while," the writer said, setting his notebook down.

"You were doing okay there for a time, didn't think you needed me."

"Don't take this wrong, but I don't think I do now," John said.

"Course you do or I wouldn't be here." He smiled boyishly. "I'm important to you. Know you better than anyone. What's that there?"

"It's called a tape recorder. I didn't have it last time?"

"My last visit? No. I'd remember that for sure," he said. "Reminds me of my roots—sounds like a sick pig."

John smiled.

"It tapes our voices, then when you play it back, you hear yourself."

"That's what you were doing when I came in—taping your voice?"

"Well. . . ."

John wanted to keep the excitement out of his voice for he loved machines and while tape recorders had been around they hadn't been easily available until recently. It was to him a new wonderful toy.

"So tell me about it."

"It's like a Dictaphone machine in that you can hear your voice. But you don't have to be close to it or speak into it like a Dictaphone machine to be recorded."

"It's a new thing in the modern world?"

"It's been around, but now it's affordable enough for people who don't have money."

"Even Okies?"

"Well, not back *then*, if that's what you mean. But now, yes, an Okie could probably afford one, if that Okie could afford a radio."

"Is it useful?"

"Yes. I read the words I have written, then see how they sound."

This thought struck the gaunt man; his posture changed and he had a look of doubt tempered by a sly smile. Having seen this often before, John braced himself.

"That so important, how the words sound? Aren't you writing the words to be read, taken in, not spoken? Do your readers read your books aloud?"

This irked the writer—the gaunt visitor had a good argument for everything. Unless he—John—was writing a play or film script, he was writing words to be read to oneself, not voiced for an audience.

"Maybe words we read to ourselves shouldn't sound good read aloud, you think of that?" the visitor said. "Maybe they're better if they're disturbing, discordant, grabbing us in an uncomfortable way, perhaps difficult to say."

"It's a thought," John said, looking past him through the window at the lights in the night. "There are writers who'd agree with you, a couple working now."

"Anyway, I know you like gadgets like this," said the gaunt man, softening. "Can it hear me and play me back?"

John stared at the reels going around. Elbows on the desk, he looked from the gaunt visitor to the machine and back.

"That's a damn good question. I wonder. . . ."

"Want to try?"

John thought about it.

"No, no, I'll wait."

"Till I've gone you mean . . . Okay, I understand—you don't want me to know."

The visitor was several inches over six feet, taller than John, and a good deal lighter, too. In recent years John had put on some weight. Of course, the visitor had the advantage of not aging; he always seemed forty-four or forty-five.

The visitor had dark eyelashes and shining dark blue eyes that seemed to express an amused if skeptical interest in life or, when downcast, a gentle melancholy, seldom anything between. He wore denim coveralls with deep pockets he pushed his hands into, and a green and white flannel shirt.

Sometimes he wore a hat, but tonight he was bareheaded or maybe, John thought, I'm just imagining him that way.

He first visited John shortly after the writer, his life threatened, left California for the East Coast. John knew his visitor was likely a creation of his own imagination, but he felt it made him question himself and accepted him as useful.

Anyway, John was pretty sure most people had such visages that came and went, if simply in nightmares and dreams, but simply didn't admit it.

Certainly many of the writers he respected seemed haunted. He felt Dickens created from personal experience when he described Scrooge's ghosts. Blake wrote of being visited by his dead brother. And several of Shakespeare's characters routinely communicated with that other world.

John noticed that if he mentioned his visitor to friends or acquaintances, almost no one would comment, would become rather quiet, in fact, or change the subject. John thought that odd because when he was a boy his sister Mary and his friends Henry and Alice loved the idea of ghosts. To kids they seemed the normal course of things and everyone either had one or had heard of one, or at least knew some good stories about a ghost or two.

In any case, it was not another world John feared, but the evil vestiges of this one. He felt it intensely in the tainted land, in houses, in small towns and large cities; to him nothing could match those moments in their bleakness and terror. Or the childhood memory of the relentless spring wind blowing up the valley, stirring the gray-green oak leaves; that, too, could be evil.

He thought of Hoover's men tailing him now, of the thugs hired to break his legs in the thirties. These were evil. Or of the afternoon in his hometown, a revolver barrel pushed up under his jaw, only terrified onlookers standing between him and his brains splattered onto the bark of an aging elm tree.

He wondered if agents, watching him from some room across the boulevard, laughed at the crazy author talking to himself. He wondered if they then reported to Hoover there was nothing to worry about, that the writer had gone round the bend. To which Hoover would reprimand them:

"Those are just the kind we need to worry about—do not let him out of your sight!"

Despite his fear, John refused to close the blinds. Often at night he went to the window and looked out, intentionally drawing hard on his cigarette so the embers illuminated his face, his graying mustache and half beard, his luminous eyes and receding hairline. He wanted to be seen in his full humanity, wearied but still creating, not beaten, a tough guy, an aging oak sheathed in strong weathered bark.

Then he'd suddenly feel again the cool of the revolver muzzle pushed up under his jaw. His toughness—that rough bark—would fall away and he'd move from the window, remembering the phone call from California, the soft voice saying someone was coming for him. That moment remained with him always, etched into his unconscious.

Looking up he saw the gaunt visitor studying him, his hands pushed into his pockets, shoulders back, his expression one of concern.

"Your work again? "

John, watching the tape recorder, the reels spinning, thought about it.

"More than that, if you must know . . . this melancholy . . . it runs in both sides of my family, creeps up on me, never know when it might . . . My father . . . a morose man . . . as a boy soldiers' funerals went by his house all day every day . . . maybe that explains it, the darkness all his life . . . Then my mother's father, a beautiful man but pretends things, creating a family of neurotics . . . "

He lit a cigarette with unsteady hands.

"Then there's me, as neurotic as the rest . . . only I have a place for my neurosis, the books—and the books become more . . . and I less. . . .

"I'd like to walk by the tide pools again, watch the little hermit crabs moving about, find a balance, a sense of proportion. But it's too late . . . no good here, no good there. I've no home, no roots, only a longing to no longer exist . . . perhaps because I have no home . . ."

Then he realized he was talking only to the tape recorder— the gaunt visitor had, as usual, dissipated before his eyes.

He stubbed out his cigarette and went to the window and looked out. He wondered—had Hoover's men seen his visitor? He crossed to the tape recorder—had the machine heard him? He turned it off. He would listen tomorrow.

Bill

BILL HAS SWEPT BACK BLOND HAIR, LAZY BLUE EYES, sucked in cheeks, a leathery look from years of house painting. He spent decades balancing on ladders leaning against collapsing gutters or rotting sideboard, but never fell far or broke a bone. He opened a sandwich shop once but that went bust and he returned to house painting.

Other than bartending two nights a week in a place called Segovia's in Monterey, in California, Bill's retired now, trying to get by on Social Security. He still drives the paint-smeared pickup truck he used in his work. Though he's working less, he remains thin, almost gaunt.

Bill grew up hearing stories about an uncle he never met, Philly fighter Eddie Cool. Eddie squandered his talent on booze, proclaiming his father died a drunk so he would, too, just to show him, and did. Bill remembered as a boy meeting the old Philadelphia trainer Sam Solomon, and crying as Solomon described the handsome Cool's demise at age thirty-five.

Bill was naturally sociable as an adult so he took a drink now and then, then a few more. He roamed the country following a stint in the Navy. In New Mexico he decided to live in Alaska and packed his pickup truck. When he hit the California coast-line, he turned north. In Monterey he pulled over and watched the waves breaking on the shore. This gave him a kind of peace. He put Alaska on hold.

He walked away from a hotel room for twelve dollars a night, got one for nine. A few days later he found a thin-walled fisher-man's cottage just above a street called Cannery Row for eighty bucks a month. Rent included a chair, a cot, a small fridge—he picked up a black and white TV at the dump.

Bill found piecemeal labor jobs. He installed braces and boards on the sides of his pickup truck bed so he could haul stuff. When someone asked him if he could paint, he did that, too, eventually graduating from interiors to more dangerous exteriors.

At a pizza bar he met an older couple, Burt and Jen, who'd been young protégés in the 1930s of a writer named John. Burt was a painter, Jen a writer. Their house up on Huckleberry Hill was often wide open for guests.

Once, not having seen him for a while, Burt and Jen showed up at Bill's thin-walled cottage with a bottle of Chianti. This surprised Burt and Jen's other friends.

"Burt and Jen don't visit *people*—people visit *them*," they said. "What's going on?"

Burt told Bill, "Do you know why we like hanging out with you? You don't treat us like old people."

Bill attributed that to his relationship with the Philly trainer Sam Solomon. He'd learned to love Sam as he'd grow to love Burt and Jen.

Burt and Jen had seen a lot of life—violence in the agricul-tural fields, John's life threatened, the much loved marine biolo-gist Ed killed when his car stalled on the train tracks. They'd seen artists and writers struggle, failures far outnumbering successes.

They'd also struggled, though recognition eventually came that was rooted in their character and perseverance as well as their talent.

Through Burt and Jen, Bill became a regular at Ed's old laboratory on Cannery Row. A kind of men's club had established itself of artists, cartoonists, judges, writers and professors. Even the business types were of a raffish bent.

Hanging over the lab were the memories of John and Ed, giving the place an exhilarating, sometimes haunted quality. People swore they got high just breathing the air, though you had to be selective—rotting kelp and dead sea life washed ashore on the rocks behind the lab and the air could be unpleasantly pungent.

That just added to the character of the place.

Eventually Bill left the board and batten cottage with the paper-thin walls and rented a larger house in nearby Pacific Grove. It was a short walk to the shoreline, a middling one to the Row and Ed's old lab. There was a big driveway for Bill's pickup truck and a shed for his painting equipment.

When a friend lost his job, Bill rented him a room in his house for almost nothing. When another separated from her husband, Bill rented *her* a room, also cheap. And so on. Bill couldn't say no. Rent included kitchen privileges as long as people cleaned up after themselves. There were pots and pans everywhere, but they sparkled.

People were everywhere, too, usually seven or eight, including a charming scholar in a frayed blue blazer living in the garage, made more habitable by carpet remnants covering the concrete floor. Bill gathered them from painting jobs especially for the scholar and his garage room.

Bill's became a social center to rival Burt and Jen's. One night the tenants and Burt and Jen were sitting around Bill's sipping cocktails while gossiping and half watching the Academy Awards. When Bill finally looked at the television, he noticed a film about a dysfunctional mental institution was winning most of the awards but its author wasn't on hand.

Bill asked Burt and Jen if, in the day, the writer John showed up when his books made into films were up for awards.

"That wouldn't have been like John," said Jen.

Burt agreed.

Bill sipped his cocktail and pondered and wondered if the writer of this story being honored was like John. He knew the author lived in Oregon. So though he realized it was a long shot, he called information. He not only got a number, when he dialed the author himself answered in his crystalline voice:

"Hello, Ken here."

Surprised, Bill said, "Bill here."

"Bill who?"

Bill said, and he didn't know why:

"Bill of Pacific Grove."

There was silence, then the writer said:

"Well, Bill of Pacific Grove, what can I do for you?"

Bill asked the writer why he wasn't in Hollywood. He'd heard he'd had a falling out with the film's producers and was that true? And how did he feel about what was going on down there, so many people except the author himself celebrating his great work of literature, now a film?

"Well, Bill of—what was the name of that town again?"

"Pacific Grove."

"Well, Bill of Pacific Grove, I'm in my backyard shed editing a magazine article so I don't know what's going on down there. But since you ask how I feel about it . . . have you ever suddenly remembered you have something important in your pocket, but when you reach in all you find is a hole big enough to match the growing pit in your stomach? . . . Well, I guess that's how I feel."

Bill felt tears coming to his eyes.

"Like after a shock treatment?" he said, trying to gather his emotions.

"Yeah, maybe so. . . ."

"Or a lobotomy?"

The writer hesitated, then said softly:

"You don't feel anything after a lobotomy, Bill—that's why they do them. But thanks for asking."

When Bill got off the phone, he confused the writer and shock treatments in his head with Sam Solomon and his Uncle Eddie Cool lying drunk in a Philly gutter. He wiped the tears from his eyes. Burt and Jen comforted him. He was becoming like a son to them.

II

BILL MET A WOMAN AND FELL IN LOVE AND THEY HAD A daughter, Lilly, and the tenants had to go. When the marriage ended tenants returned, old and new ones. A few had died. Lilly, as she grew to young womanhood, usually had six or seven adults looking after her and getting in the way. Sometimes, in the mornings, she helped pack lunches for those who worked.

Meanwhile, life at Ed's old lab was changing because Cannery Row was changing, helped along by a series of mysterious fires that leveled old canneries and opened the land to development. The historic value of the canneries became a moot point once they were gone, and as a bonus a few developers saved the expense of razing the buildings.

Land cleared, work began on a sprawling luxury hotel then was stalled by money problems as a recession set in. Cyclone fences were erected around the site to wait out the bad times but couldn't hide concrete pilings and rusting rebar.

The lab guys as well as merchants and restaurant owners didn't mind eyesores from the past littering vacant lots. Fish hoppers and caved-in boilers had character and echoes of John and Ed, of fishermen and burned down canneries. They were good for business. Recent pilings and rebar weren't, lacking the color and character age bestowed.

Someone had the inspiration of hiding the new mess with murals depicting Monterey history and life. With the city's encouragement and financial backing, Burt put out word anyone with the artistry and vigor to paint murals of Monterey's past and present was welcome to try, all materials supplied. There began a great cultural and artistic movement that soon consumed Monterey and the surrounding communities.

The city provided a hundred large plywood boards and Burt coerced Bill into priming them on the lab's back deck, hiring an attractive masseuse to keep Bill and other volunteers supple and on the job.

Bill tumbled off the masseuse's table when a major earthquake struck on a fall afternoon and some of the already installed murals collapsed. But they were repaired and nobody on the Row was killed and, most importantly, the lab held together.

The mural project miraculously transitioned from an attempt to artistically cover up pilings and rebar into a universal symbol of the rebuilding spirit of mankind. Burt was lionized. A walkway leading down to the lab was named for him and nothing could have pleased him more.

Not long after, Burt and Jen's house burned down. Burt gathered himself for a final project—designing and constructing a new house for Jen. As with the murals, there was no shortage of volunteers to help. When the house was completed, Burt declined quickly.

On his deathbed, Burt said to Bill, "I love you—Jen loves you—John and Ed would have loved you. You are part of the legacy." Then, asking Jen and Bill to lean closer, he whispered, "Please, I don't want to be mourned—dance in the streets all night long."

The city shut down Cannery Row traffic in Burt's honor. With floodlights highlighting the murals and the lab, people danced all night to band music, none longer than Bill. The party brought back memories of John and Ed and the old days.

Jen went on for another decade. She worried to friends that often, when Bill called late at night to talk about Burt and the old times, he'd had too many cocktails. It tore at her heart. Bill wondered about this because when he visited her, he said, it was usually Jen who "toted out the Jack Daniels."

Both were lonely.

III

ON A RECENT WINTER AFTERNOON, TWO MEN KNOCKED on Bill's door. They were wearing suits, loose ties and carried clipboards. They showed Bill identification. The heavier one said, "We're from the city. We've had complaints. Your tenants are living here illegally, have been for years. They have until four this afternoon to vacate the premises."

The other said, "You know, Bill, these aren't the old days anymore. Not the '30s and '40s you seem to think you're living in. Those people are dead and those days long gone. You need to let go."

Bill nodded, then worried about the scholar in the frayed blue blazer living in the garage. Over the next few weeks Bill helped find shelter for all of his tenants. A friend invited the charismatic scholar to room with him across town. Lilly was already independently in her own place, so that was not a concern.

A few weeks later, Bill was evicted from the house. He moved in with his daughter. Depressed, he drank a little. Memories of old Sam Solomon's stories of Bill's uncle Eddie Cool were always there to make him think hard. He would push it to the edge, but never cross a line he had firmly set in his head.

Even when Burt and Jen had worried about him in earlier times, he knew he would be okay. He would not die in some gutter like Eddie Cool had in Philly. If he hadn't learned abstinence, he had learned a kind of control.

But he knew he had to leave. He could no longer afford the region's rising living costs. He cast about. One night he had a dream, fondly remembering a dusty border town in New Mexico he had paused in during his travels as a young man. He had been happy there for a time.

He made calls, talked to people, even a realtor. He was told he could live cheaply in this town, which had changed little in the decades since he'd left. It seemed his kind of place. He found, for very little, a miner's hut facing out over the desert.

So he made the move. Like the sound of the breaking waves, the desert silence brought him a kind of peace. And like his first home in Monterey, the miner's hut had paper-thin walls. Bill settled in.

Publisher's Postscript

STEINBECK: THE UNTOLD STORIES IS THE FIRST BOOK PUB-lishing venture of SteinbeckNow.com, an educational web-site devoted to the life and writing of the twentieth-century American author who continues to attract an international readership, inspire new art, and inform public discourse about twenty-first-century issues with life-and-death implications. Four of the sixteen stories published here first appeared online, in earlier versions, at SteinbeckNow.com. So did a pair of plays by Steve Hauk that, like his Steinbeck stories, capture the California spirit of place and possibility celebrated in Steinbeck's fiction from *The Pastures of Heaven* to *East of Eden*.

Steinbeck: The Untold Stories was a natural choice when the decision was made by SteinbeckNow.com to begin print publishing as a service to the international Steinbeck community. Steve Hauk's fiction brilliantly fulfills the website's mission to stimulate fresh thinking and new art. It also establishes a standard of performance for future volumes of creative and critical writing about Steinbeck, an international artist who struggled to find an audience until he was discovered by the Romanian-American editor and publisher Pascal Covici. The striking illustrations created by C. Kline for Steve's Steinbeck stories—like the characters in "Olie," "Judith," and "Burt and Jen"—remind us that Steinbeck moved happily among painters, musicians, and other creative types during the often-unhappy life re-imagined in *Steinbeck: The Untold Stories.*

Marny Parkin of Orem, Utah, provided inspired guidance and instant execution in designing the book's interior, and Kathleen Burgess, a poet and editor from Chillicothe, Ohio, corrected textual errors with an eagle eye. Dixie Layne's concept for the cover, featuring C. Kline's expressive portrait of John Steinbeck, was carried out with input from Scott Eurich of Wilesmith Advertising | Design in West Palm Beach, Florida. It's easy to imagine Steinbeck approving fault-free, long-distance collaboration like this, based on individual experience and generous give and take. A solitary worker who was fortunate in his friends, he died before digital technology made efficient, economical publishing more than a poor writer's dream. Unfortunately the cost of academic and trade books today has pushed them beyond the budget of a majority of the readers he wanted to reach: young people and adults with the curiosity, empathy, and emotional intelligence to participate in the stories he had to tell. The website dedicated to an author who insisted on accessibility is pleased to publish affordable books inspired by his example.